Invisible Girl

Also by TESS HUDSON

DOUBLE DOWN

And writing as ERICA ORLOFF

DO THEY WEAR HIGH HEELS IN HEAVEN?
MAFIA CHIC
THE ROOFER
DIVAS DON'T FAKE IT
DIARY OF A BLUES GODDESS
SPANISH DISCO

Tess
Hudson

Invisible Girl

MIRA

ISBN 0-7783-2314-5

INVISIBLE GIRL

www.MIRABooks.com

Printed in U.S.A.

With great love, to my mother, Maryanne

ACKNOWLEDGMENTS

A long time ago I was befriended by a Vietnam-era veteran who taught me a great deal about writing and art and even faith. I was an impressionable twenty years old at the time, and I glimpsed a different side of the war from what I remembered on the evening news when I was a little girl. I owe a great deal of the imagery of this book to Ed. Far away, but still in my thoughts.

As always, I thank my agent, Jay Poynor, for his support. And I especially must thank, from the bottom of my heart, my editor Margaret Marbury. For some reason, I have never written about the mother-daughter relationship, always choosing in my books to write about fathers and daughters. Margaret urged me to add the character of Mai, and when that happened, it was like a dam bursting. This novel is really the story of mothers and daughters and bonds that are never broken.

I must thank my own mother, whose friendship is one of my adult life's most precious gifts. I also pause to remember my grandmother, Irene Cunningham, whose absence never stops being a great emptiness in my heart. I also want to thank Alexa, Nicholas, Isabella and Jack...by loving my children so totally, the story of Mai was able to come to life.

My father...somehow his stories of Manhattan are always interwoven in my books. This one is no exception.

My sister Stacey Groome is one of my biggest cheerleaders. She has read every one of my books, and I am so lucky to have her as a friend.

Other family and friends: my sister Jessica, Kathy J., Kathy L., Nancy, Cleo, Pammie.

I'd like to acknowledge the wonderful team at MIRA, my publisher. I especially love my cover. Thank you to Sasha Bogin for her insights and editorial direction, and for her enthusiasm for this book. And the members of Writers' Cramp. I began this novel three times, always agonizing about weaving the past and present. Jon, especially, encouraged me to travel deeper into the past and into Vietnam and Laos as I wrote, and the book is better for it.

Finally, I would like to acknowledge J.D. He patiently let me read aloud to him, and felt every tear and heartbreak that my characters did. I love you.

If a man speaks or acts with an evil thought,
pain follows him.
—Buddha

In war, truth is the first casualty.
—Aeschylus

We will not learn how to live together in peace
by killing each other's children.
—Jimmy Carter

How could man rejoice in victory and delight
in the slaughter of men?
—Lao Tzu

I'm fed up to the ears with old men dreaming up wars
for young men to die in.
—George McGovern

Prologue

To Mai, the East River was as mysterious as the moonlit river near her childhood village in Vietnam, but it was colder—and more dangerous. In New York, she didn't need to fear snipers or a sudden assault from American helicopters, like hawks circling above, waiting to swoop, the smell of napalm burning. She needed to fear the river itself, as if it were alive, living, in the way Buddhists taught that all things were living and connected.

Mai knew no single current controlled the river, no orderly flow ordained by the moon and the tides. Instead, currents fought against each other, colliding and viciously warring with each other, waiting to pull anything into the river's depths. Beneath the surface were cars and old appliances, trash, worn tires, the silt making visibility impossible. NYPD scuba divers who came to search for jumpers couldn't see their own hands inches from their faces. Mingled in the waters, too, down in the silt, were bodies. Murder victims and jumpers in the East River were as much a part of New York lore as alligators in the sewer system. Mai knew bodies lurked.

No one survived the East River. No one. The currents would drag a body down deep, as if claiming it for some unseen angry god. She feared the bodies. The dead luring her, their skeletal fingers beckoning, whispers in the night, *join us.*

Mai tried not to think of her children. She longed for a last hug, to hold them tightly on her lap and breathe in their innocence. She felt her resolve weakening. Then she pictured Jimmy. He was her brave soldier, her hero, and from the first day she saw him appear through the tall reeds into her village, she loved him. Thoughts of Jimmy, of his fearlessness, like a tiger in the grass, stalking, patient, courageous, filled her.

The air whipped at her silk dress, the one he loved best, and her hair, long and black, flew about her face. She almost lost her balance. Then, with a mournful glance skyward, she whispered.

Forgive me.

And Mai Malone, her thin body lithe and graceful, arms stretched wide, stepped off the pier and into the ebony waters swirling below her.

Chapter One

Clinton.

Not for the first time, Maggie Malone shook her head in wonder at how trendy Hell's Kitchen had become. They'd even rechristened the area Clinton, after DeWitt Clinton, a New York governor from over a hundred years ago. Everyone knew Clinton Court and the old DeWitt Clinton school, but face it, Maggie thought, the name Clinton allowed real-estate developers to make this part of the city sound more attractive. Who wants to pay a million dollars for a co-op in Hell? The yuppies had invaded like bacteria spreading through an infected sore. They made Clinton fashionable. But for her, it would always be Hell's Kitchen.

Emphasis on *Hell*.

Down at the end of the bar, a guy with an expensive haircut waved an American Express platinum card and snapped his fingers. Maggie took her time strolling over to him and the three girls—two brunettes and a blonde, all in low-slung jeans and expensive tops—hanging all over him.

"I'd like a bottle of your best champagne," he said loud enough for pretty much anyone in the bar to hear, though the crowd was thinning out.

"First, we don't carry champagne, and second, we don't take AmEx."

"Fine, I'll put it on a different card."

"We don't take cards, period."

"What?" He looked at her incredulously, then he shook his head. "Fine. Give us four sour appletinis."

Maggie gave a slight nod and moved down the bar a couple of feet to mix the neon-green concoction. When she'd been a little girl, the Twilight had been a hellhole. You didn't even walk in if you weren't neighborhood. Not if you knew what was good for you. She'd started out running the register, standing on a wooden crate. Her brother Danny had cleaned tables. They'd both graduated to bartender before their eighteenth birthdays. But back then the drinks had been beer, bourbon, scotch, vodka, boilermakers. Not appletinis and cosmos.

The yuppies had started coming in a few years before. Danny was rude to them. Maggie was ruder. She felt desperate to hold onto the Twilight the way it was. The way it had always been. Her familiar alcoholics. The ones she drank with, the ones she threw out at 3:00 a.m. The ones who knew her father.

She served the appletinis and then went down to the far end of the bar to refill the beer in front of Charlie—no last name that she knew of—an old-timer.

"What's eatin' you, Maggie? You look like you lost your best goddamn friend."

She shrugged. "I just hate seeing the place like this."

"What? Crowded? Making money hand over fist?"

"You know what I mean," she snapped at him. His nose was like a road map of crisscrossed blood vessels, and he had a way of curling over his beer, lest someone should steal it.

"So sell."

"I keep thinking about it. Got another offer this week. Haven't talked to Danny yet."

"What's the old man think?"

She shrugged. "We haven't heard from him in months."

"Wanna know what I think?"

"Sure."

"Sell the fuckin' place. I don't know what the hell you're holding onto it for. Take the money, go retire to friggin' Florida or something. Get out of the winter. Al Roker said it was minus ten with the windchill this morning. That's colder than a witch's tit."

"Point taken, Charlie." Maggie noticed how the spittle gathered in the corners of his mouth, and his teeth were stained with tobacco, like the ceiling of the Twilight itself. He was one of the last of the old-timers. They were dying off.

God, despite its patina of hopelessness, she loved the place. In the midst of Hell's Kitchen, it was her oasis. Her temple and shrine to all that she loved.

They raced into the Twilight.

"Hi Daddy!" Maggie squealed, both her front teeth missing. He picked her up and kissed her nose, depositing her on a bar stool and filling a highball glass with Coke.

"Don't tell your mother I'm giving you Coke. If she asks, tell her I gave you milk."

Danny climbed up on the stool next to Maggie. Their father tousled Danny's hair and poured him a soda, too. Then their father leaned two elbows on the bar and asked them about their day.

A few stools away from Maggie, she noticed a man with prison tattoos on his forearms. She waved at him, and he winked at her.

Danny told their dad about his class's field trip to the Museum of Natural History. Maggie couldn't wait to be in third grade and take that trip, too.

"Dad…the elephant had tusks that went up to the ceiling!"

"Did it try to eat you?" their father joked.

"No. It was stuffed."

"Oh…well, you two better get upstairs to Mom before she stuffs the both of you. Finish your sodas, and no telling."

Maggie dutifully sucked the last of her Coke through a straw, slid down from the stool, and ran back outside with Danny to the double doors leading to the apartments above the bar. They took the stairs two at a time to apartment 2B.

The door was open before they even got there. "Take your shoes off!" their mother scolded them.

Maggie, in the tartan plaid skirt, blue kneesocks, white blouse and blue blazer of Saint Bernadette's Catholic School, complied and slipped off her Mary Janes. Danny untied the laces of his shoes. He wore his blazer but had loosened his tie the second the last bell had rung.

Only with shoes off did they run into her arms.

"How was your day?" she asked them. Her accent made

her cut the endings off words sharply, slightly. "You have good day?"

They both nodded.

"Come." She took them each by the hand and led them to the shrine to Buddha in one corner of the living room. A white altar cloth covered the table. A pewter bowl contained fruit, an offering for him. A vase held flowers.

Out of habit, in the ritual they did each day, Maggie and Danny bowed deeply. Then they lit incense. It was Maggie's turn. She withdrew an incense stick—jasmine-scented—and took a wooden match and lit it.

"Thank you, Buddha, for my good test score in science, and for Mark Callahan getting the chicken pox," Maggie said.

"Why you thank Buddha for that?" Her mother asked.

"'Cause then he wasn't in school to pick on me. He pulls my hair."

"Oh," her mother said and smiled. "Your turn Danny."

"Thank you, Buddha, for my trip to the museum. I got to see a woolly mammoth."

They bowed again with their mother. Maggie loved their Buddha shrine. They had a few statues of him, some solemn and meditative, but one was a big, fat Buddha with a round belly. She liked how happy he looked, like he was laughing.

"Come," their mother commanded. Next they moved to a small shrine of Jesus and Mary, the Blessed Virgin. "You tell him thank-you. Thank his mama, too."

So they went through their thank-yous again, this time adding an *Our Father* and *Hail Mary*. Maggie didn't like praying to Jesus as much. Compared to Buddha, he was sad, his statue plastic and in Technicolor, with painted-on red blood dripping from his palms and feet and side. The stations of the cross at St. Bernadette's were even more graphic—to remind the children of our Lord's pain and suffering, said Sister Patricia.

Maggie had never told the Carmelite sisters at St. Bernadette's about Jesus and Buddha being best friends, according to her mother. "Best to cover all your bases," her mother had said. "Keep you safe." Somehow, Maggie didn't think the sisters would approve of covering their bases.

Maggie, Danny and their mother made the sign of the cross. Then it was homework time. Around five, Maggie's father came up from the bar for his dinner break. That was always her favorite part of the day. Not because she got to see him and spend time with him, although that certainly pleased her. It was the strange thrill she got from watching her father walk through the door and the expression on his face when he saw her mother.

Maggie tried to capture the moment in her mind, but it never was the same as seeing it, being there with them. But Maggie was convinced the earth stopped moving—just for a split second. He opened the door, shut it, took off his shoes, lined them neatly next to Maggie's and Danny's. Then he came into the dining area, and when he first caught her mother's eyes, it was there—you could feel it. Her mother's breath left her and her father's heart stopped. Maggie was sure of it.

Her mother was always calmer with Daddy around, certain they would all be safe now. She would serve him supper, but she always made sure to touch his hand, to rub his arm as she put his dinner on his plate. And Maggie's father would not curse, he wouldn't raise his voice, not even a tiny bit. He wouldn't do anything loudly. For that time, that meal, he was under her mother's spell, and they weren't in Hell's Kitchen. They were someplace else. They may have been above the roughest bar on Thirty-ninth Street, but inside was a piece of heaven, watched over by Buddha and his brother, Jesus—because, Maggie's mother said, someone as wise as God would have a lot of children.

Maggie walked away from Charlie and prepared to break down the bar. It was late; she was tired. The phone rang, and she picked up the extension by the register.

"Angel?"

"Hi Bobby," she said.

"I'm just getting off work. I caught a case. Some guy killed with a pickax. There's no end to the creativity in this city."

"You sound tired."

"I am. I was thinking of coming by, though. I just need to see you."

"Sure. I'll be here."

Maggie hung up and continued breaking down the bar. She had the lone cocktail waitress start stacking chairs on top of tables. The loudmouth with the three girls wasn't taking the hint, so Maggie raised the house lights and turned off the music. Finally, the creep raised his hand and wrote on an imaginary check in the air.

"Thank God," she muttered.

She took his money, gave him his change, sent Charlie home and told the waitress she could go. She collected the tips on the bar—the rich guy had left her a single dollar.

Charlie, who lived from disability check to disability check, had left her a five.

She was alone. She went to the register to count the till. On top was a big happy Buddha. He smiled at her and she at him. She rubbed his belly for good luck.

Next to the register, taped to the mirror behind the bar, was the first twenty-dollar bill the Twilight had ever earned. It was signed by Uncle Con, who, as the story went, had bought her father a shot of bourbon to celebrate the opening. He'd then signed the bill and up it had gone. Next to that was a photo of her father and brother and her from three years before. Danny was smiling; she was open-mouthed, squealing with laughter. Their father had just told them a dirty joke and someone had snapped the picture, right there behind the bar of the Twilight.

She hadn't heard from her father in a while. She hadn't seen Danny in three weeks.

The worry made her want a drink.

She looked at Buddha. "What cosmic mind fuck has a recovering alcoholic owning a bar?" she asked him. Then she patted his belly and poured herself a Coke and waited for Bobby to come. He was the one, and they were right for each other. Like her mom and dad. Every time she saw him, she felt the earth stop for just a moment. When he was near her, she felt safe.

Chapter Two

Danny Malone felt around his mouth for the loose tooth. It was the last molar on the right, and if he moved his tongue against it, the thing wiggled, the unique, slightly salty taste of blood intensifying. He couldn't use his right arm at all. He guessed that shoulder was dislocated. With his left hand, he felt his face and discovered it had the texture of raw hamburger meat.

He slumped over in the driver's seat of his somewhat battered Lincoln Town Car. The pain was so bad he felt as if he were going to pass out. He looked up at the six-story red brick building and could see the light on in his sister's apartment on the second floor. All he had to do was get up there. *Just get to her, Danny.* Like a penitent man on a pilgrimage, he thought only of reaching his Mecca. The one place where his world made a little sense.

All his life, Danny's sister Maggie had fixed everything. He was older—by two years and change—but she was the one who kept out of trouble—and tried to keep him out of trouble. She was like their mother. After their mom had died, Maggie had been the one to retain the rituals, the Buddha, the crucifix. She was the one who made sure he and his father ate home-cooked meals and had clean clothes.

Danny's head pounded and he struggled to focus. From the time they were little, Maggie would check out all his scrapes and bruises, surveying the damage. Once they were teens, and then adults, she would look for more serious scrapes. Like bullet holes and knife wounds.

She was like his other half. Anyone with a set of eyes could see they were related. They both had the same jet-black hair, which sometimes, in the right light, took on a bluish sheen, black eyes, slightly almond-shaped and exotic, and pale skin. He was well built, muscular, and had a pair of dimples that belied his toughness; she was delicate, with high cheekbones that carved out hollows beneath them, just like their mother, and hair that fell nearly to her ass. His nose had been broken twice, so it leaned a little to the left, but they were clearly siblings.

Danny opened the car door with his functional hand and climbed out, slamming the door behind himself. He looked up and down the street through the slits of his swollen eyelids. He turned up the collar of his army jacket—his father's old one, threadbare, with an ancient maroon-brown stain of blood on the arm, either his father's or a Vietcong's. Danny knew if anyone saw his face, he'd scare the shit out of them, and they'd call the cops, so bending his head into the wind, he started toward his sister's building.

Each step sending shock waves of pain through his body, he made it to the building's heavy door and then up to the second floor and her apartment—2B. He fiddled with the lock, pulling the copy of her apartment key from his pocket.

Suddenly, the door flew open, a male voice shouted, "Freeze, asshole," and a gun was pointed at his head. He saw Maggie, her beautiful face ashen by the sight of him. He pulled his collar down, letting her fully see his face—what was left of it. She screamed, and then Danny knew he could safely give in to the pain. He fell to the floor and let sweet oblivion overtake him.

Maggie knelt on the floor by her brother, oblivious to the blood that was smearing the flannel pajama bottoms she had just changed into. She took his head in her lap and cradled it, brushing a lock of blood-soaked hair from Danny's face as she rocked ever so slightly.

Bobby Gonzalez shouted at her to get away. "You don't know who this fucker is. Call 911. Jesus Christ!" He kept his gun drawn.

"No!" Maggie looked up at him, her chin quivering. "This is Danny."

"Your brother?"

She nodded.

"Christ!" Bobby put his service revolver back in his ankle holster, his hands shaking from the adrenaline rush, and leaned down next to her. "He needs an ambulance." Bobby put two fingers on Danny's neck, feeling for a pulse, then reached for the cell phone at his waist.

"No." Her voice was etched with panic. "No, no… Look…I don't know why he's in trouble, and I can't really explain it all right now, but you have to trust me. I have to handle this here at home."

"*Handle* this? Angel, we need to get him to a hospital and then find out who did this to him. You can't take care of this. You're in shock. Look, just stay calm and let me call an ambulance."

Maggie recognized his "cop voice"—authoritative, soothing in an emergency, talking to her as if she were a child. "No…look, I'm begging you. *Begging* you. Please let me take care of this."

"Here? Jesus, Maggie, what are you talking about?"

"I don't have time for this, Bobby." Her voice careened and changed to one hostile and strong, equally authoritative.

"Fuck! This has to do with your family shit."

Maggie nodded, wincing a second at Bobby's anger. "Stop being a cop for a minute and be my friend. Help me." She looked up into his face. His eyes were so dark, she couldn't see the pupils for the irises, and she watched him clench and unclench his jaw, then pass his hands through his hair. He paced back and forth a few times. Finally, his anger seemed to be replaced with worry.

"Maggie, what kind of trouble is your brother in? What kind of trouble are *you* in?"

"Please… We can talk more when he's in better shape. I need boiling water. I have a sewing kit in my bedroom closet. Gauze and tape in my bathroom closet. I…think there's an Ace bandage in there. Towels. Um… Shit…um, I need rubbing alcohol. Neosporin." She tried to picture her medicine cabinet, mentally scanning each shelf from left to right, to see what she had that could help Danny. "Oh, and there's a bottle of Tylenol No. 3, top shelf, medicine cabinet. I need that and some applesauce and two spoons."

Bobby looked at her. "You're serious about this."

"Look, please just do what I ask and I swear I'll tell you everything later."

He hesitated, then finally stood and walked past her and Danny. Maggie heard Bobby rummaging through closets and the medicine cabinet, slamming doors, spilling things onto the floor, hurrying. He returned with most of what she asked for and then went to boil water in her small kitchen.

Maggie looked down at Danny, who was unconscious. She wondered if kitchen-table stitches were anything like riding a bicycle, that once you learned how to do them, you never forgot. It wasn't all that different from sewing cloth. And the Malone men were never ones to worry about leaving a scar. She told herself it would all come back to her.

She was fourteen, and after Jimmy Malone had locked up the bar, he called upstairs to their apartment. She answered on the first ring.

"Mags?"

"Yeah, Daddy?"

"I need you to come down to the bar. Danny's doing some things for me…won't be home until late."

Things. Maggie knew that could mean anything from driving out with Uncle Con to New Jersey to bury something, to hiding money in a hole in the wall behind the toilet where there was a loose tile. It also meant not asking questions.

"Be right down."

The Twilight bar was in Hell's Kitchen, which itself was bound by the Hudson River. Eventually, if you walked west, you'd hit the water, as black and ugly and foul-smelling as it was. When she was very little, she'd imagined the Hudson River as the sea, mystical and grand, carrying the scent of fresh water and the sounds of sails whipping into the wind. But she was older now and realized it was just the dirty, brown Hudson. Hell's Kitchen's other border, depending on who you asked, was Eighth. Either way, it was a haven for the Westies and addicts, and the streets were harsh. But Maggie had never felt unsafe. She knew everyone in a thirty-block radius was aware of her father's power in the small jungle of their neighborhood. He'd fought two tours in Vietnam, and some people said he'd flown for the CIA in Laos. Or maybe it wasn't for the CIA, but for some shadowy arm of the government that had condoned paying him $10,000 cash each month back in 1973. Maybe he'd flown for Air America. That was the rumor, at least, and she had no reason to doubt it, collecting small clues like a hungry bird snatched up bread crumbs. She stored the information away in her mind, hoping to one day understand all that her father was. After he'd come back from Laos, some of the money—from whoever had paid it to him—had gone to buying the bar.

Maggie's teeth chattered. Her father's mysteries always made her nervous. He was the antithesis of what she remembered of her mother. Where she embodied the rituals of incense and quiet and candles, her father and Uncle Con immersed themselves in the never-spoken threat of violence—not against her or Danny or her mother when she'd been alive, but against anyone who dared to even breathe on them. Maggie pulled a sweatshirt over her head and looked around her bedroom. The far wall was lined with shelves on which perched at least a hundred Buddhas, maybe more. Some had been her mother's, some her father had bought her in Chinatown. And some, she knew, came from faraway places in Asia from before she was born. On the opposite wall was a crucifix, a pretty wooden one with a pewter Jesus. On her dresser were the spilled secrets of a teenage girl—hair clips, lip gloss she had just been allowed to start wearing, earrings and rings and fortune-cookie promises of good luck and prosperity, movie stubs and cutout pictures of movie stars she planned to stick on her bulletin board.

She took a deep breath to settle her nerves and left her bedroom and then the apartment, locking the door behind herself. She descended the metal staircase to the back entrance of the bar, the scent of beer as familiar to her as her own name, as her reflection in the mirror.

Maggie walked through the back of the bar and then made her way to the cluttered office, where she assumed her father would be waiting for her. He was, though he was slumped over his desk. He looked up, with effort, as she came in the door.

"What's the matter?" she asked, even as she saw the wet crimson stain on the back of his shirt.

"Nothin'," he said, winking at her, his face sweaty and ashen. "I just need you to do me a favor, baby girl, and dig this stupid thing out of my shoulder, out of my back."

"What stupid thing?"

"A bullet. I'd do it myself if I could reach, but I can't."

Maggie felt queasy, not because he'd been shot, but from the idea of sticking a knife, tweezers, anything, *into* a hole in someone's flesh, let alone her father's.

"Daddy…" she said in a whisper, laden with the question, there in the way she spoke his name, *do I have to?*

"I can't ask Danny. He's doing something for me. And I can't get Uncle Con on the phone. *Please*, I'm asking you. I'm starting to run a fever, and I've got to get it out of me. I'll talk you through it. Piece of cake. You're a Malone."

Maggie nodded. "Are you going to be okay?"

"I promise. And you know I never promise unless I can deliver the goods. Please, baby."

She breathed deeply, not sure if she would pass out or not. "I'm going to get me a drink."

"Sure. Get me one, too."

Maggie went out to the bar and pulled down a bottle of scotch. She took two fat water tumblers and set them on the bar. She hated scotch. Although her father had let her and Danny drink beer since they were small, she never drank anything uglier than peppermint schnapps. But she wanted something powerful and nasty. She poured two generous scotches as if she were pouring water. She took one and downed it in a few gulps, fighting the retching feeling in her throat and gut, emitting an audible gag. She put the tumbler on the bar and literally shook her shoulders and head, trying to keep the vile liquid inside her. Then she refilled her glass and brought it along with her father's drink into the office.

A first-aid kit was open and his shirt was off. The kit looked like an army-issue one, and she imagined it had come home from Vietnam with him, long before she had even been born.

"Thanks, darlin'," he said, taking the scotch from her and downing it without shivering or even making a face.

Maggie stood behind him, staring at the bullet wound. Its edges were clean, and it looked deep. She could only see dark red blood, but she knew that in the hole, layers of skin gave way to muscle and below that bone. Steadying herself, she peered into the hole of flesh and blood, smelling the bitterness of burned skin, again feeling a violent convulsion in her stomach.

On her father's desk was a scalpel. A real scalpel, not a knife. She didn't ask where he'd gotten it or why he had it. She never asked about anything. Not about the loaded gun that always sat on his nightstand, or about the occasional 2:00 a.m. visitor, men with whispered secrets and file folders and photographs. Next to the scalpel was a pair of very long tweezers with pointed ends.

"Okay, Maggie," he said as he handed the scalpel to her. "Now, the scalpel is really sharp, so don't cut yourself. Just poke this into the hole and dig out the bullet a little. Use the tweezers when you can finally see it. Get all of it. Make sure of that. If it's hit bone, you'll have to dig more."

She gritted her teeth, hands shaking. Gingerly, she entered the back of his shoulder with just the very tip of the scalpel, feeling as if she were going to throw up.

"Honey, don't be afraid to hurt me. I've taken way worse." He laughed. "Ain't nothin' to an old soldier like me."

By now, the scotch was having its effect. Feeling as though she were in a dream, watching someone else stick a scalpel into the wound, she dug deeper, blood oozing from the hole and dripping in small rivulets mixed with sweat down his back. She finally saw the bullet's gray-black color. She switched tools, and Maggie's tweezers emerged minutes later with the bullet, which she scooped into her hand and then placed on the desk. Her father visibly relaxed, his back tense from effort of steeling himself against the pain.

"Now the stitches."

He talked Maggie through cleaning the wound with peroxide, which sizzled and bubbled. Then she sewed the edges of the wound, packing gauze into it, and then covered it with a large square piece of gauze, and finally she taped all around it.

When she was done, her father turned around. He had the solid jaw of a soldier. His eyes were a peculiar blue-green, nothing like his children's. His hair was a dark shade of brown, speckled with a little gray. Freckles scattered across his nose and deep lines surrounded his eyes, from squinting, he'd told her once, as he'd marched in the sun. His body was still as taut as when he'd been in the service, with rock-like biceps covered in tattoos, and then the old scar from the war. She had pictures upstairs of him in the grassy fields of Vietnam, a youthful soldier, but still something about him, an air of toughness, that came through even in the grainy photographs. He looked nothing like Danny and her. They would always look, to strangers, like adopted children, their features so much their mother's.

"I'm sure you left a pretty scar." He winked at her. "A new one that I'll always know you fixed up."

"Are you going to tell me what happened, Daddy?"

"Nope. I'll tell you what, though… Did I ever explain why I named this place the Twilight?"

"About a hundred times."

"I know. I just like that story."

"I still like hearing it."

"Well, then. It was because in Vietnam, twilight was beautiful. I mean, we were in a shit hole of mosquitoes and humidity, but that sky turning orange and pink sometimes, it was…humbling. And off in the distance, it's like you'd hear fireworks. Of course, it wasn't fireworks. It was war. I used to watch the burst of flames rising up from the treetops.

"For pilots, twilight can be dangerous. Sort of that world between night and day. Between heaven and hell. I didn't think I could feel that *aware*, every muscle twitching. And one twilight, we'd landed near this village. It seemed okay. Peaceful. I waded through the swamp, and me and my guys, we walked toward some huts, and I saw a girl carrying a basket. She was the most beautiful girl I've ever seen in my whole life. And in that second, in that minute, my whole world changed. Vietnam went from being a place I hated to being the place where the person I loved was from. When I finally got back to America, I bought this place and named it after my alive time, when I realized I never wanted to live so much as when I saw her. Twilight. When the sky was pink."

"I wish I knew you then," Maggie whispered. She wished she knew him now. He was her father, but he was a stranger.

"I remember the day you came home from the hospital. I was alive then." He shrugged his shoulder a bit, moving it around. "This is gonna be a bitch tomorrow."

"Sure is." She grew silent for a minute. They both did. "Okay then," she said softly. "I'm going back upstairs."

"Thanks, kiddo. You really came through for me. I love you, bright eyes."

"Love you, too."

She left the office and grabbed the bottle of scotch off of the bar, taking it with her to their apartment. As soon as she got up there, she ran to the bathroom and threw up, the scotch burning her throat a second time as it seared her on its way out. She leaned her elbows on the toilet seat and felt her lids fill with tears, but she refused to cry. She stood and washed her face in the sink. The hole in her father's shoulder kept coming into her mind. She left the bathroom, took the bottle of scotch and put it on the dining-room table. She fetched a mug from the kitchen and began drinking, forcing herself to keep it down, drinking the hole of flesh away. That night was the first time Maggie ever drank herself into a blackout.

"You're making me nervous," Maggie snapped at Bobby, who leaned over her and was staring at her handiwork, occasionally offering advice.

"How did you learn to do that?"

"It's like riding a bicycle."

"Sure it is. Only you would use that analogy."

Danny's face now vaguely resembled Dr. Frankenstein's monster. Black thread wove crookedly through loose skin, but she had closed up the slice in his cheek, cleaned off the blood and sewn up the cut above his eye—it was deep and ran through the eyebrow. She bandaged his arm, hoping perhaps it wasn't a break, but setting it as best she could. She had tried to jam the dislocated shoulder back into place the way she'd seen her uncle Con do once for her father.

She applied a warm washcloth over and over again to

Danny's face, slowly easing off the caked blood. She cleaned along his hairline and wiped his hair. He looked better than when she'd first seen him. Swollen, turning an eggplant-purple, but with some of Danny's "luck o' the Irish and blessings of Buddha," as their mother used to say, he'd still have a semi-beautiful face when it was all healed.

Maggie mashed some Tylenol No. 3 into the applesauce and roused her brother enough to feed him three tablets. Then, with Bobby's help, she got him onto the mattress they'd taken from her pull-out couch and had placed on the floor.

"Now we watch him," she whispered, getting up from her makeshift operating room.

"Your hands are shaking."

"The first time I did this, I had half a bottle of scotch in me. Actually, the second and third time I did this, I had scotch in me."

"Drinking wouldn't have made this night any easier."

"Easy for you to say."

"Look, Maggie, I just watched you stitch up a man on your living-room floor like you work in a fucking MASH unit. I'm part of this whether you like it or not."

She sat down on the love seat, and Bobby took the chair opposite her.

"I'm sorry, Bobby."

"Don't be sorry. How about telling me the truth? Let's start with that."

"Truth depends on who you talk to. But I know I owe you as much."

Maggie looked down at her hands and tried to decide where to begin.

Chapter Three

"Courageous and crazy. It's a volatile cocktail. That's my father. That's my brother. My father was drafted during Vietnam. He became a pilot. He tested so high, they'd never seen scores like that. He's smart, with nerves of steel. Courageous and crazy, both of them."

"I know a few cops like that."

"He's always been like that. My dad has two brothers. One was murdered after a stint in prison, and was supposedly as violent as they come. The other is the dean of Manchester University in Boston. He has two PhDs. They were like the twin sides of my father. Brilliance and violence. And secrets."

"Secrets?"

She looked at Danny. "It's as if there was a different life before the war. And then there's this brick wall of Vietnam. He ended up volunteering for another tour. We know he met my mother there, and that he somehow got her out. Danny and I think he was recruited into the CIA."

"What do you mean you 'think'? You never asked him?"

"We don't ask a lot of questions in our family. But even if we did, he wouldn't talk to us. The CIA was involved in Laos after the war, during the war. My father flew planes for them—for someone. Someone with a lot of cash. You know, the CIA isn't the only secret branch of the U.S. government. It could have been them, it could have been another shadow organization. It could have been Air America. All I know, which is nothing, just street knowledge from this neighborhood, is that he was pulling in a lot of untraceable cash from some government organization that wanted missions flown in Laos. And they were willing to pay a crazy-courageous man a lot of money to risk his life over and over and over again."

"He made it out alive."

"Yeah. But I'm not sure that he ever made it out," she said softly, her eyes darting to Danny, almost involuntarily.

"What do you mean?"

"My whole life, my father has been a phantom. I don't know whether he works for the good guys or the bad guys, or if he plays both sides, or whether he just works for himself. When my brother got to be, I don't know, seventeen, eighteen, he started getting in deeper with my father. But I was always invisible, always on the outside of whatever it was that they did, whatever it is that they do."

Bobby leaned back in his chair and ran his hands over his face, giving a weary sigh. "So what happened to your brother tonight, Maggie?"

"I don't know. I don't know who did this to him. I don't even know if he started it or not."

"Have you ever told your brother not to come to you

when he's in trouble, not to drag you into whatever crazy shit he's involved with? For all you know, it's drugs or murder for hire. You don't know anything, Maggie. You could be in danger. Whatever he and your father are into, they shouldn't be putting you in the middle of it."

"I know, but they're all I've got."

"You have me."

"I know," her voice relaxed. "But growing up, this apartment was a place where only good things happened. It was like us against the evil spirits my mother was always talking about. This was a place just for the four of us, and I knew that my father would kill anyone who tried to mess with us, with our sanctuary. After my mother committed suicide, my father went crazy for a while. He never got over it. None of us did. But it only made us closer. I don't know what my father does. Maybe because I don't really want to know."

"That's pretty severe denial."

"You're not my shrink."

"No," he said as he leaned forward and looked her in the eyes. "Do I really have to be to see that there's something very seriously fucked up going on here? You *stitched* up your brother. And you don't want to file a police report or take him to the hospital?"

"You don't know what happened, Bobby."

"Maggie, don't play me. Even if Danny didn't commit a crime tonight, the fact that you apparently have done this for him and your father more than once…that's not normal."

She curled her legs underneath herself. "I'm tired, Bobby. Can we just talk about this after I'm sure he's going to be okay?"

"You're putting this off again, Maggie. I've been with you for two years now, and I feel like I know next to nothing about you. I've never met your brother until now. I've never met your father. It's like I'm living with a phantom of my own."

Maggie looked away. "I've lived a lifetime of secrets. It's like lifting up a rock in the woods and watching all those creepy-crawlers scatter when the light hits them."

"Fine. You go get some sleep. I'll watch your brother."

"No. You sleep. Please. I wouldn't be able to anyway."

Bobby nodded. "I'll be right in the next room. You call me if you need me. And look…we don't know how much blood he's lost or what's up with that arm. If he doesn't seem like he's going to pull through all right in the next couple of hours, we're taking him to the hospital." He was silent for a minute. "I'll try to pull some favors, see if we can't keep it under the radar."

"Thanks." Maggie smiled wanly. Bobby walked over and leaned down, tilting her chin to kiss her.

"I wish I knew what went on behind those eyes of yours."

"So do I sometimes. Good night, Bobby." She kissed him back and watched him go to the bedroom. He was the first good man she'd ever dated. She'd known that the first time she'd met him, as surely as she knew one day his world would come colliding with hers with a fury like nuclear fusion.

Two years earlier, she had quit drinking, cold turkey, on her own, white-knuckling it. For three days, she'd ridden out the shakes and the endless clenching and unclenching of her jaw by eating Valium she'd taken from her brother's stash of drugs in the medicine chest. They all hoarded pills from years of "home repair," as their father called their questionable medical skills.

By day three, the Valium had done its trick. She had slept until she ached, and she was through the worst of it. She sat in her apartment in the dark, staring at the emergency bottle of scotch. She had brought scotch up from the Twilight, an old habit. She hated scotch and had figured that if all she had was something she truly despised, she'd be less inclined to break the seal. She had brought it upstairs with the idea that if quitting got truly unbearable, she'd change tactics and wean herself slowly, decreasing her intake of alcohol day by day until she was clean.

Now, she had gone without alcohol for three days. Three whole days. Not great days, glorious days, or even halfway decent days. Three of the most god-awful, soul-sucking days of her life.

A thought came into her mind: AA. She'd never been to a meeting, not even out of curiosity. She knew a regular or two at the Twilight who were in and out of AA, on the wagon for months at a time, falling off when life just got too damn hard. Teddy, a good guy, a plumber, had a son die about five years past. He walked a wobbly line, not unlike the straight line cops made people walk to see if they were drunk. Some days, Teddy walked it well. Others, he just plain toppled off to the side and lost his balance completely.

Maggie sat in her apartment and, for reasons she didn't understand, she felt tears come. They weren't like her occasional drunken tears. These came with a racking ache. So she picked up the phone, called information and, the next thing she knew, she was at a meeting in a church basement not eleven blocks from her apartment. The first person who said hello to her was Bobby Gonzalez.

"New to the rooms?"

She never liked admitting being new at anything to anyone. "No. First time here, though."

"Bobby." He stuck out his hand and smiled. He was about six foot two, and dressed in a black sweater and jeans. She took his hand, looking into his eyes, searching for something. Later, she realized it was the elusive serenity they talked about in the rooms and basements of AA meetings. Did he have what she was looking for? The secret to peace of mind?

"Maggie."

"Hi, Maggie." He seemed so gentle. He directed her to the coffee urn and poured her a foam cup of the worst coffee she'd ever tasted in her life. He chatted about the program. She didn't really remember much of what he said because she still felt like she was under water, foggy. Then he guided her to a metal folding chair. Bobby took a seat at a table at the front of the room, next to an older man. The older man, who said his name was Gus, started the meeting off, and Bobby was the speaker.

"Hi, my name's Bobby," he began softly, "and I'm an alcoholic."

"Hi, Bobby," came a chorus of a voices.

Maggie listened as he spoke.

"Most of you know me from the rooms. I've been coming here about ten years, sober for eight straight. I'm a cop, a detective. I used to think it was my job that made me drink. Now I realize I drank because. Just because. Because I'm an alcoholic.

"I started drinking when I was maybe eleven, copying my older brother and his friends. But they were typical teens looking to be cool, to rebel a little. I wasn't. I couldn't stop drinking once I started. I had my first blackout at fourteen. Smoked a lot of pot. I was a mess through high school. By the time I was twenty, I knew something was seriously wrong. I became a cop, met a lot of alcoholic cops. Man, if you're looking for validation for your drinking, law enforcement is one profession you'll find it. Everyone needs a drink to settle down after a tough night, a tough call, a tough tour. You see the worst, the dregs. You see wife beaters and child abusers and rape victims. I needed a drink to shut my brain off at night.

"So why did I get sober? I hit bottom. I got lucky. I didn't think I was lucky then, but I was. Everybody has their bottom—DUI, jail, divorce, whatever. Mine was waking up with a prostitute and having no memory, none, of what happened the night before. I felt such a sense of shame that I went to my first meeting that day, and then that night, and then the next day. I screwed up a couple of times early in the program, but then I got it. It's one day at a time. I get that now. That and the promises of AA. If you get sober, life gets better. I went back to school, made detective.... I have so much more now than I ever did before. I'm not going to mess up. Thanks for listening, and now we'll go around the room and share."

There were about forty people in the room. They applauded. Maggie felt mesmerized, and she wasn't sure why. His voice was soothing. He looked so confident, so calm. She wanted that.

She listened to others share, thankful they ran out of time before they got to her. After the meeting, Bobby approached her.

"Um, do you want to get a cup of coffee? I usually go to a coffee shop a few blocks from here. It's open until four in the morning."

She smiled. "Okay."

They walked together to the Blue Moon Diner. They didn't say much, but the way they walked, they fell into a rhythm with each other, finding a stride. The diner had a bell that jingled over the door when they opened it. The tables had little jukeboxes on them, and they sat in a back booth. He put quarters in their jukebox and played some Elvis.

She stared at him across the table. She was pretty sure she looked like someone who'd just white-knuckled it for three days, but she was grateful Bobby hadn't seemed to notice.

Their waitress came over, and Bobby ordered their coffee. When it came, Maggie wrapped her hands around her mug, hoping the heat would calm her.

"Much better coffee than at the meeting," he said as he leaned into the table and smiled at her.

"You can say that again." She sipped the coffee. "And you remembered—two sugars and lots of milk."

"I'm a detective. I'm paid to notice details like that." He winked at her. "How come I've never seen you before?"

She looked down at her coffee. "I'm…kind of quiet. I blend in."

"You don't blend in anywhere. I spotted you the moment you walked in."

"Well, I go to meetings all over. I haven't really picked a home group."

"I almost always go to the one at St. Michael's. And I pick up a lunchtime meeting in Manhattan sometimes."

"A cop, huh?"

He nodded. "Does that turn you off? A lot of women just don't want to date a cop, or even be friends with a cop. Too stressful."

"Doesn't bother me."

"What do you do?"

"I'm a bartender."

"You're kidding."

"Nope."

"Isn't that kind of hard with your sobriety?"

"Not really." She wasn't about to admit her "sobriety" had lasted all of three days.

"Well, I guess you must be able to twelve-step a lot of people."

She looked at him blankly.

"You know, refer a lot of people to the program. Talk about the steps."

"Um, yeah. Mostly I listen to people's problems. Bartenders are paid to listen as much as pour drinks. So…do you like being a detective?"

She had a bartender's psychology, a way of asking a question and then shutting up. Most people, she had come to discover, weren't really looking for a bartender's advice any more than they expected a shrink to tell them what to do. They just wanted to talk out whatever it was that was bothering them.

Sitting in the diner across from Bobby, his life story spilled out in more detail, and he told her about being a detective, about what drove him. "My best friend was shot when I was twenty-two. We were together at a bar down in lower Manhattan. He walked one way, I walked the other and went home. He ended up dead. Luck of the draw, I guess. His wallet was missing. Maybe it was a mugging gone bad. They never caught the person who did it, and I have this feeling like he's following me all the time. Until a case is solved, that's what ghosts do, you know. They follow you."

"You believe in ghosts?"

He cleared his throat. "Not like seeing spirits and stuff, but I feel like the soul isn't at rest until the case is solved. Do you believe in ghosts?"

"I think so." She thought of her Buddhas and lighting incense and speaking to her mother. She thought of how her father was a ghost even if he was flesh and blood.

They talked—Bobby doing most of the talking—until after midnight. She found being around him comforting.

"I don't want to say good night," he said as he helped her from the booth. Their waitress had been sighing each time she passed their table, and they knew they'd overstayed their welcome. Maggie watched him put down a twenty-dollar tip, and as a bartender, she appreciated someone who did that. Their bill was less than nine dollars. He'd ordered a slice of pie.

"Me either. I live near here. Do you know the Twilight?"

"Rough place."

She laughed. "I own it. Well, my father does. I live above it. If you want, I can make more coffee." She looked at him intently, willing him to come, not sure why she was so drawn to him.

"Sure."

When they left, a winter chill blasted them and, almost involuntarily, she leaned toward him, nearly against his arm. They walked the twelve blocks or so to the Twilight. At some point, he grabbed her hand. It was an intimate gesture, holding hands tightly, as if they were a couple.

When they got to her building, she opened the door and they climbed the stairwell to her apartment. She unlocked the door and moved to the side to let him in.

Turning on lights, she said, "I'll make some coffee."

"To be honest, I'm all coffeed out. If I have any more, I'll never get to sleep."

"Okay. Would you like a soda? Water? Juice?"

"Nah." He took off his jacket.

"Here, I'll put it on the coatrack." She took his jacket from him and hung it up, placing hers on the hook next to it.

She turned around and looked at him, feeling peaceful for the first time in days, but now nervous. He walked closer to her and put his hands on either side of her face. Without saying anything, he leaned down and kissed her gently. She kissed him back.

The next thing Maggie knew, they were moving toward the bedroom. She felt as though she wanted literally to pull him inside of her, as if she wanted to hide within him, to find refuge somehow in that calm voice of his. The sex between them, even though he was a stranger to her, was incredibly intense, leaving her breathless and holding onto him.

"I wish I knew why I… I never do this," he said. "I just felt like I knew you."

"Me, too," she whispered. He was in no hurry to leave. An hour later, they were making love again, and he curled himself around her, holding her tight to him as they fell asleep. She slept without Valium. She slept without dreaming, which was the point, she guessed. Dreams were always scattered, uneasy images to her.

In the morning, she rolled over and watched him sleep. There was something angelic about him, innocent. It was something missing from her father's face, from Danny's. The minute Bobby opened his eyes, he grinned widely. "I was hoping I wasn't dreaming about last night."

They stayed in bed, made love, and had coffee and eggs and read the paper.

"This is kind of crazy," he said, sliding under the covers after breakfast and clutching her to him, her head nestling perfectly against his shoulder. "Getting involved so fast. They tell you not to do that in AA."

"Sometimes you just know."

She never told him she was embarking on day four without alcohol. After that night, they rarely slept apart. And Maggie rarely craved alcohol after that. Bobby was her pacifier. He was the way the night made sense.

Chapter Four

Saigon, June 11, 1963

Mai Hanh's mother grabbed her daughter's hand and urged her along the crowded street near the opera house. They made the trek to Saigon once a year to shop for a few items and to visit Mai's aunt, who had left their village with a Frenchman some years before and now lived in an apartment that Mai thought smelled of a strange mixture of clove cigarettes and dumplings.

The streets were filled with pedestrians, and Mai frequently bumped into people as her mother tugged and pulled, demanding her to walk faster than her ten-year-old legs could carry her.

Ahead of them, an enormous gathering of people stood, blocking the way, as they formed a circle. Mai couldn't see what was going on, but she heard chanting.

"Ma, what is it?"

Her mother, who usually walked with her head bent forward and down, as if expecting to confront a strong wind, lifted her face. Mai noticed how tired her mother appeared. She was always tired when they visited *Tante,* as her aunt insisted Mai call her. *Tante* wore a silk dress the color of emeralds, stiletto heels and stockings with a black seam down the leg, red lipstick, her hair in intricate braids with tortoiseshell combs. Ma wore plain black pants and a loose top, both made of coarse cloth and flat black cloth shoes. Ma never wore lipstick, didn't own lipstick, and the years of working in the fields had taken their toll on her hands and the skin on her face.

"I don't know," Ma said.

Mai craned her neck but saw nothing but the backs of the people in her way. Then she decided to crouch. From her new vantage point, she could glimpse the center of the circle. Crouching further still, she saw Buddhist monks and nuns. They were speaking about charity and compassion.

"What is it?" Ma asked, looking down at Mai.

"I don't know. Monks." Mai squinted as an elderly monk with a smooth face sat down, his saffron robes gleaming in the midday sun, his eyes serene and determined. The nuns and monks around him were speaking, reciting from books, but Mai couldn't make out what they were saying. The sitting monk remained calm. Tranquil. Mai watched as they poured a liquid on his robes and then his head. Something was shouted from the crowd and she heard a scream.

The sitting monk set himself on fire. They had been pouring gasoline, Mai realized as the intense smell of burning flesh assaulted her nostrils.

"Ma!" She grabbed at her mother's legs and clung to her,

unable to look away from the image of the burning holy man, waves of nausea sweeping over her as her stomach fell and shuddered.

"What is it, Little Mai?"

"He's on fire, Ma."

Her mother quickly swooped Mai into her arms, though Mai was too big to be held like that anymore, and her spindly legs trailed down her mother's body. Protectively, her mother pushed Mai's face against her shoulder, forcing Mai to look away.

"Why, Ma?" Mai cried, tears rolling down her face.

Her mother shook her head. "Vietnam is like grain that the hens peck. First this one wants her, then that. France, America. Pecking at us. Pecking."

The crowd had grown restless and angry over the immolation. Mai's mother insistently pushed and maneuvered until they were down a side street, moving away from the commotion.

Later that night, Mai tried to sleep. But in the flames of the cooking fire, she kept seeing the monk. She wondered if Buddha had given him the courage. Because even as he'd burned to death, the monk her mother said was named Thich Quang Due had never flinched. He had burned alive without moving a muscle, without uttering a single cry of agony.

Chapter Five

Sometime near dawn, Maggie watched as her brother stirred. She crossed the room to his side and knelt down.

"Danny?"

"Hey," he said, squinting up at her, his voice hoarse and gravelly.

"Want a sip of water?"

"I'll take a shot of J.D. if you have it," he said as he winked his good eye.

"No, you won't. I'll get you some water."

She stood and went to the kitchen, returning with a small glass of ice water. She helped Danny lean up on the elbow of his good arm so he could take a sip.

"Hope I didn't scare you too much."

"I'm used to it by now."

"Yeah, but last time you told the old man and me you'd had enough of this bullshit."

"I was angry. Forget about that. How do you feel?"

Danny leaned back down on the mattress and felt along

his face, his fingers tracing the ragged line of the home-sewn stitches. "I bet as bad as I look. Even my eyelashes hurt, bright eyes. My earlobes hurt. There's nothing on me that doesn't hurt."

"Want some more Tylenol with codeine?"

"Yeah. But I better eat something with it. Toast."

"How's the arm?"

"I don't know. I'm not sure if it's broken."

"I think it was just a dislocated shoulder. I hope it was, at least. You going to tell me what happened?"

"Damned if I know."

"Come off it, Danny."

"I'm serious. Three guys came into the warehouse we got out in Jersey. I was just getting ready to lock up. From the looks of them, I knew they didn't want a pirated DVD."

"Have you ever seen them before?"

He moved his head very slowly from side to side.

"You owe any money around?"

"I've been laying off the betting. Nothing. I got a bad feeling as soon as they walked in, and I started to walk toward the desk, where I keep a gun in the top drawer. One of them, a huge cement wall of a guy, blocked my way."

Maggie winced. "Christ, I know where this is going."

"Exactly. They locked the door and beat the living shit out of me. I put up a fight. Smashed a chair on somebody's head. But three guys, Mags. I didn't stand a chance."

"And did they tell you what they wanted?"

"No. They just kept saying I knew what they wanted, which I didn't. They flipped the warehouse from end to end. Went through my lockbox. They didn't take the cash or find what they were looking for, either. They left me half-dead on the floor and said they'd let me think about it, and that they'd be back. I barely remember getting up and driving here."

Maggie's teeth started chattering from nerves and she pulled her knees close to her chest as she sat on the floor. "You have *no* idea who they were?"

"No. But they mentioned Dad. And from how they looked…you know the type."

"Christ, what is he into this time?"

"I have no idea, and if we don't figure it out, I'm a dead man. And frankly, I'm not too sure you're safe, either."

Bobby Gonzalez's deep voice called out from the bedroom doorway behind them. "What do you mean Maggie's not safe?"

Maggie startled and whipped her head around, and then she turned back and exchanged a look with Danny.

"Listen, if you two are in trouble, I can help."

"Maggie told me you're a cop. And cops, in general, don't help the kind of trouble we're in," Danny said.

"And what kind of trouble is that?"

Danny glanced at Maggie. "It has to do with our father."

"So ask him. Whatever these guys wanted, find out what it is and give it to them."

"We can't ask Dad." Maggie didn't look directly at Bobby. "We don't know where he is. He took off over a year ago. He wouldn't say why. Said it would be safer if we didn't know where he was. We didn't ask questions."

"What kind of father leaves his kids in danger like that?"

"We're not kids. We can take care of ourselves," Maggie snapped.

"As evidenced by you having to stitch your brother up last night? Look, if you don't want to report this, fine, but I hope you have a better plan than sitting here waiting to be killed for whatever it is these jerks wanted last night. What'd these guys look like anyway?"

Maggie saw the answer in Danny's eyes before he even said anything.

"Feds," he whispered.

"What was that?" Bobby came closer to the two of them. Instinctively, Maggie touched Danny, as if he were a talisman of reassurance. She fingered his shirtsleeve, almost absentmindedly.

"Feds," Danny said again, louder this time.

"I don't get it. What are feds doing beating the crap out of you?"

"Whatever our father did in Laos," Maggie said, "he had friends in high places." She paused. "And enemies in even higher places."

"So we put out feelers. I can find someone to trust in the bureau. We can get to the bottom of this discreetly, put you into protective custody if we have to."

"You don't get it, pretty boy," Danny said, shutting his eyes. "You won't find our father anywhere in the bureau, or anywhere, period. He doesn't exist."

Bobby looked at Maggie, who nodded in agreement. "You could reach out all you want, Bobby. He doesn't exist. He's a phantom, and by birthright, so are we."

Maggie watched as Bobby's eyes revealed a struggle to understand. He paced back and forth a few times before he turned back to them. "I don't accept that you're just going to stay here and wait for them. You have to be able to do something."

"We can call Uncle Con," Maggie suggested.

"Who's he?"

"Our father's best friend," Danny replied.

"And he'll know where your father is?"

"Maybe. We have another uncle, Dad's brother. He lives in Boston. But Con is more likely to know where he is."

"What's Con short for? Conrad?"

"No. Con artist."

"This just gets better and better."

Maggie got up to go make Danny some toast. As she neared the kitchen, Bobby approached her. "Can we talk in private?" he asked.

She followed him into the bedroom and shut the door.

"Are you out of your mind?" he asked her.

"No."

"What's going on?"

"I don't know."

"You have *no* idea?"

She sat on the bed. "From time to time, men would come to the Twilight. They looked like CIA. Feds. I didn't ask questions. Then maybe two or three years ago, things started to seem dangerous. I can't put my finger on it, but my father changed. He began moving things to safety deposit boxes. Became paranoid, which wasn't like him. Maybe *paranoid* isn't the right word…just very secretive."

"Sounds like the guy was already pretty damn secretive."

"This was worse. Then he took off."

"Just like that?"

"In a way, yes." She looked up at Bobby, aware for the thousandth time since their first night together that he was good in a way the shadowy world of her father would never be.

"I don't know what to say, Maggie. Let's call this uncle Con of yours and see what he thinks."

Maggie went to the phone, then thought better of it, not wanting to use her land line. "Can I use your cell?"

Bobby picked up the phone, which was next to his wallet on the dresser. He handed it to her.

Maggie dialed the number, praying Con would answer even if he didn't recognize Bobby's number on caller ID.

"Yeah." His voice came over the line in the vaguely hostile way he had of answering the telephone.

"Con, it's Maggie."

"Oh, bright eyes, I'm so sorry."

"You heard about Danny?"

"Danny? No. Don't tell me those fucking bastards got to him, too?"

"Too?"

"Is he dead or alive?"

"Alive, but just barely. What are you talking about Con?" Fear seeped into her voice and around the edges of her brain. Bobby came and stood behind her, pulling her backward against his chest and wrapping his arms around her.

"Your father, Maggie. I thought you knew."

"Knew what?" she asked, but felt the answer down in her stomach, in the way it tightened.

"He's dead. The bastards finally got him."

Chapter Six

Our Father who art in heaven...

Jimmy Malone was surprised at how quickly the words leaped to his tongue. The short one, the one with the bad teeth, kept poking at Jimmy's broken arm. Tears of pain filled his eyes. The short one poked harder, his finger touching bone through the deep gash that ran from Jimmy's elbow to his shoulder. The short one said something unintelligible to the taller one with the lazy left eye, and without even knowing their language, Jimmy could tell they were angry.

Bile rose in his throat. Six months ago, out of shame or politeness, he would have turned his head. Now, sweating in the jungle, insects swarming around his eyes, making blinking a necessity to ward off insanity, he merely leaned forward and retched from the pain. He felt his own vomit warm the front of his shirt.

Hallowed be thy name...

The prayer was there. On the edge of his consciousness. He repeated it over and over in his mind. A mental salve on the open sore of being twenty-two and hopelessly bent and broken in a jungle farther from New York's west side than he had ever imagined he might go. Farther than he'd ever wanted to go.

Thy kingdom come...

Sometimes Jimmy thought about the words.

Thy will be done...

How could this be God's will? This war, his arm, the short one with the bad teeth. The hunger. The bugs. The fucking bugs. *God, how can this be your will?* Death. Cowboy Mc-Mann blown to smithereens right in front of him. The land mines. The bugs. The infection spreading up his arm. Malaria. *In two days, I will be dead. If I make it that long.* God's will. Jimmy wanted to weep, but that wasn't how he was raised—his father would have just as soon punched him in the face than allow a son of his to cry. His mother was the same, a tough old woman, always a bourbon away from passing out.

On earth as it is in Heaven...

Hell. *Fucking hell. Hot as hell. That's what this place is,* he thought through the pain, so intense at times he thought he was floating above himself. When had the short one left? He couldn't remember. It all ran together. Day and night. Bugs and stickiness and pain and bugs all the time. Same day. Different day. All the same.

And lead us not into temptation...

And sometimes he didn't think about the words but just

the sound of them. Like a mantra, he repeated the prayer. *I am still alive. I am still alive. Our Father. Our Father. Our Father. I am still alive.* Not that he was sure being alive was a good thing. Dying far from home on the floor of a hut, gooks poking him, swollen mosquitoes too fat to fly from drinking the blood clustered on his wound. Young North Vietnamese— no more than boys—hitting him with sticks. All he could think of was relief. Death or rescue. One way or the other. Relief.

But deliver us from evil…

And that line, when he thought about it, was for the Washington assholes. The politicians whose own sons would never see the war, or if they did, it'd be as paper-pushers somewhere. *Fucking evil motherfuckers. You come die here.*

Amen… Fucking evil.

He tried to imagine the antithesis of evil. He thought of Mai. He had a rule when he was flying. He wasn't allowed to think of her. Men died when they let down their guard, fragments of thoughts of home or their girl making them careless. Instead, he put Mai in a box in his mind. Then, when it was time, when he was on the ground, when he was safe, he would shut his eyes and open the box and take her out.

Their moments together were rare. It was hard to get away, to get to her village. And she came to Saigon infrequently. But when he saw her, Vietnam was bearable. He couldn't believe he was content to do as little as hold her hand. But he was. He liked to bring her things to make her smile. An American camera, candies, bottles of Coca-Cola, a Timex watch. He kept a picture of her inside his helmet.

Mai. His Mai. She was smiling at him in the picture, sunlight on her face. He would look at her photo and almost forget the war. Maybe what she said about Buddha and reincarnation was true. Maybe he'd known her in another life.

He hoped she was safe. Mai's father was dead. Killed a year ago. Determined to keep Mai from harm, Jimmy had brought some buddies and they'd dug a hiding spot big enough for her and her mother and baby sister in case their village was raided. Between the hiding spot and the money Jimmy was able to give Mai, he'd even won over her mother. He wished this fucking war would be over and he could bring them all to America.

Jimmy thought of Mai and the pain eased a tiny bit, replaced by an ache in his heart. He would never see her again. Sometime between dusk and dawn, in the darkness, the rats came. He named the first one, a fat son of a bitch, Cass, after Mama Cass, and he felt a twinge of pride at his bravado. Humor in the face of an amazingly hopeless situation. When the second and third and fourth rats showed up, a tidal rush of pity and fear swept over him. Cass bit his ankle. A second prayer entered his mind.

Hail Mary, full of grace...

Then he abandoned the prayers and spoke to God from the very depths of his soul. He spoke with the abandon of an angry man, not much out of his teens, in despair. Without artifice. Without bargaining. He had nothing to offer God. He whispered in the darkness. *God, if you get me out of this fucking shithole, I'll do something with my life.*

In a flash, an explosion rocked the earth and sent the rats scurrying. Gunfire, screaming. The sound of choppers in the distance. The ground beneath him shook, and he screamed as his arm jostled. But God—or Mai's Buddha—had just delivered Jimmy Malone his first miracle.

The door to the hut flew open. The jungle was on fire. The short one had returned with a large knife.

No! Not this way! Please…

Gun blasts. The short one's eyes bulged, his face illuminated by orange flames behind him. He fell forward. Dead. God's second miracle.

Two Americans burst through the door, guns in hand. They saw Jimmy tied to a wooden post.

"Holy Christ. Get him, Mac. I'll cover the doorway."

The one called Mac cut Jimmy free. "Buddy, your arm's in bad shape. What's your name, soldier?"

"Malone," he managed to shout above the sound of gunfire. Then he saw stars as the circulation of blood suddenly returned to his mangled arm. From somewhere far away, he heard himself scream, and then he passed out cold.

He was lucky. He wasn't going home missing a limb, like some freak. His face was still good-looking, he had all his limbs—he'd go on to fight another day…back in Hell's Kitchen

He was lying in bed, squeezing a tennis ball he'd somehow managed to trade for a pack of smokes. He squeezed it with his bad arm maybe ten thousand times a day as he listened to the morphine-addled screams of other patients.

Sometime near midnight, as he lay awake, a shadowy figure approached his bed.

"Malone?"

"Yeah?" He looked up at the tall man, whom he didn't recognize, the man's face backlit by the bare bulb in the hallway.

"You up for a walk?" His accent was homegrown U.S. of A.

"Sure," Jimmy said, lengthening the word with uncertainty.

Jimmy climbed out of bed, leaving the tennis ball on the mattress as he followed the American man out into the hall and then downstairs into the courtyard. He had no idea who this guy was, but something about him spoke of power, as if he didn't hear the word *no* too often.

In the center of the courtyard, the man turned to him. "I hear you have steel balls. You're scared of nothing."

"Have we met?"

"No."

"Well, where the fuck did you hear that from?"

"Fingers O'Reilly."

"What the fuck?"

Fingers O'Reilly wasn't in Vietnam. Last Jimmy had heard of him, he was in Sing Sing Correctional serving ten to twenty for armed robbery and assault with a deadly weapon.

"Do you?"

"Look pal, do I what? What's with the head games?"

"Do you have steel balls?" The man was dressed in khaki pants and a white cotton shirt that looked custom-tailored. He had silver hair and the coldest eyes Jimmy had ever seen— a pale gray. His face was unlined, tanned, strong looking, with a scar on his left cheek that looked like a tiny sunburst.

"Maybe. Listen, you see this arm? It's my ticket out of this fucking hellhole."

"What are you going back to? You don't have a girl back home. She's here."

Jimmy fought his temper. Whoever this asshole was, he knew a lot about him, so he wasn't going to ask how he knew. He wouldn't give him the satisfaction.

"So what? I'll get her home somehow."

"Not likely. Not in this political climate. And what are you going back with?"

"What do you mean? I'm going back with both my fuckin' testicles, all four limbs, and my mind, which is more than I can say for most."

"How'd you like to go back with a few hundred thousand dollars?"

"Yeah, okay. You've been here too long pal, whoever you are."

"I have a proposition for you." The man didn't smile. Jimmy realized he also never said what his name was. "I have an offer to make you, Malone. A gamble, if you will, for a pilot like yourself. Maybe a quarter million in untraceable money"

"U.S. dollars," Jimmy said disbelievingly.

"Yes." The man still didn't smile. "Cash."

Jimmy didn't speak for a long time. He could hear the honking of car horns and the noise of soldiers out in the streets on R & R. He looked up at the night sky, and then finally turned to face the man in the shadows of the courtyard.

He took a calculating breath. "I never said I wasn't a gambler."

"Excellent," the man replied. "That's exactly what I heard." Then, for the first time since he'd appeared on the hospital ward, the man grinned. But Jimmy noticed the smile never reached his eyes.

Chapter Seven

Bobby had a headache. It was concentrated on the right side of his head, near the temple, then snaked up around the top of his skull and down the base of his neck. His temple throbbed. He never used to have headaches. Not even when he was a drunk and woke up each day shrouded in the fog of a hangover. But ever since he'd met Maggie, he'd started getting headaches. Often.

When Maggie's uncle had delivered the news that her father was dead—murdered, according to Con—she had crumpled to the floor in slow motion. She didn't cry. Her mouth moved, but no sound came out, and she rocked back and forth for a while.

Bobby had knelt down next to her, pulling her to his chest, and then she'd whispered, "My father's dead."

He'd stroked her hair, not really knowing what to say. He knew her father was a Vietnam vet and that he owned the bar. He knew even less than that about her brother, until he'd shown up the previous night, his face smashed in.

Now Bobby was following Maggie's directions and taking her and Danny to Con's house, which Maggie said was down in Jersey somewhere, out in the backwoods, down a dirt road. A dirt road that was booby-trapped.

"I'll tell you how to get around the traps," she said, patting his leg as he drove, as if this were the most normal thing in the world. His headache, which was a dull throb, started to pulse with more intensity.

Bobby glanced in the rearview mirror. Danny was leaning against the window, mouth open, sound asleep after a tall shot of Jack Daniel's and three Tylenols with codeine. Danny hadn't blinked when Maggie had told him about their father, but looked resigned, as if he'd half expected it. Danny was pale, and Bobby guessed he should have had a transfusion or something. What the fuck did he know? He wasn't a goddamn doctor, but a cop—who was now driving his girlfriend to some booby-trapped old farm down in Jersey.

"What does your uncle need booby traps for?"

"To keep poachers away," she said calmly.

His head throbbed more. She could lie so easily that if he didn't know better, he'd swear she was a sociopath. She'd been lying since the moment he'd met her. She'd tried to give him a line of shit that she'd been in AA a while, had some sobriety under her belt, but he was certain she hadn't been telling the truth. He'd seen her hands shake those first few mornings he'd slept over. He'd seen her in the bar where she worked, the look of longing in her face for a drink, almost a hungry look. The longing in her eyes had disappeared eventually, but he knew she wasn't as strong in her sobriety as he was.

He stared straight ahead at the road. It was a windy fall day, gusts of air occasionally swirling amber and gold leaves onto the highway. He thought back on his first encounter with Maggie. In all the years since he'd quit drinking, he hadn't had a vice. He didn't smoke. He didn't gamble. He didn't sleep around. Then he'd met Maggie and, inexplicably, she'd become his one obsession. Because whenever he was with her, he had this ache that started in his chest—that sometimes wormed its way upward and turned into a headache later—but an ache to make love to her, and to keep her safe. He wasn't sure how he knew she wasn't safe, but he just did. Cop instinct, he figured.

The lying... The lying made him angry, worried. He tried to imagine what sort of trouble she was running from and if it would land on her doorstep with a thud in the middle of the night someday. He didn't have to imagine what that would be like anymore.

He glanced over at her and wondered for the millionth time why she didn't trust him, why she appeared to have no past, when he knew it was there, waiting to overtake them, like the shadow of a bogeyman creeping into the bedroom. And he wondered why he wouldn't leave her, as sure as he knew the booby traps on her uncle's farm weren't for poachers.

After a while he spoke, eyes straight ahead at the road. "Poachers?"

"Hmm?"

"Your uncle booby-traps his farm to keep poachers away? Isn't that kind of extreme?"

"Maybe. I never thought of it that way."

He knew this was a charade. She was playing him. Poachers? More likely other men like the ones who nearly killed her brother. "What are you going to do about your father? A funeral and everything, I mean."

"Nothing."

"Nothing?"

"Daddy never wanted a funeral, or a memorial. He wanted to be cremated, quickly. Before they burn him, he wants us to put rice and some money in his pockets."

"Rice and money?"

"A Vietnamese custom, except they sit with the body in Vietnam. Still, he said the rice was to feed you on your journey to the next life. Same with the money, to pay your passage."

"And he believed that?"

"No, he didn't. I don't think he believed much of anything. But he found it comforting. Rice and money. Rice and money," she whispered, her voice trailing away.

"I still don't understand what's going on, Maggie. Who attacked your brother? Who killed your father? Leaving me in the dark isn't accomplishing anything. I can't protect you that way."

"You can't protect me anyway."

"Why not?"

"Because to protect someone you have to know the enemy. You have to be ready for him. And I don't know the enemy. They're shadow people. Even Con doesn't know."

"You want to tell me the whole story?"

"I don't know it all myself. But Con, he'll tell us what he knows."

Bobby's head continued to throb. She was rubbing his thigh, and despite the headache and her beaten-up brother in the back seat, he was aroused. Her touch did that to him, which made him more annoyed with himself. Her fingers slid over to his cock and started rubbing up and down the zipper of his jeans. He glanced at her face, and it was blank, as if she was doing this, touching him, absentmindedly, from instinct. He didn't stop her and tried to focus on the road. About five minutes later, she abruptly stopped and pointed at a turnoff, "Head down there."

The turnoff was a single lane of blacktop heading well off the rural highway they had turned on a while back. After driving through woods for another few miles, Maggie pointed at a fallen log. "Stop there."

He stepped on the brakes.

"You have to move the log. It's hollowed out, not too heavy."

He looked at her for a moment and put the car in park. He climbed out and moved the log, seeing that a road stretched behind it. Maybe *road* wasn't the right word. It was a deeply gutted path, worn by tires, so that you could follow it through the woods. Some loose gravel was scattered about, and that was it. He couldn't imagine what her uncle did when the snows were heavy in winter, but then again, judging by what little Bobby knew, Con didn't take much to having visitors.

Bobby climbed back in the car. Maggie was gently rousing Danny, whose glassy eyes and pale face still weren't looking too good.

"Is he running a fever?" Bobby asked Maggie.

She put her hand to Danny's forehead. "Mild. Low-grade." She seemed satisfied with that and smiled at Danny, then turned around to face front.

"You're going to follow this for exactly one mile. *Exactly.*"

Bobby drove slowly, the car bouncing over the mounds of dirt. Bobby could see Danny grimace with every bump. When the odometer clicked over to one mile from where they'd started, Bobby stopped the car. They had already passed two signs stating Trespassers Will Be Prosecuted.

"Make a left," Maggie said.

He turned his head. There was nothing to the left but ferns and dead leaves.

"Where?"

"There's another road past that bush. It's all fern. A few branches might scratch the paint, but you can drive right through."

Sighing, he made the turn and, as they passed through the ferns, his tires found the grooves of another path.

"Follow this for a mile."

He did as she instructed, and this time she told him to make a pass to the right. Then he followed the dirt and gravel of the path for a few hundred yards until he could see a log cabin, smoke billowing from the chimney. He parked the car and leaned over and kissed Maggie on the lips. Whatever was in the log cabin, whatever he was going to find out, he loved her. Lies and all, he loved her.

Chapter Eight

Maggie ran from the car to Uncle Con, who'd come out of the cabin at the sound of their arrival. She buried her face, just for a moment, against the shoulder of his worn jacket. When he had returned from Laos with her father, he had refused to wash the army field jacket. In fact, he had never washed it as far as Maggie could tell. Her father said a lot of Vietnam vets didn't wash the mud or blood from their boots or uniforms. It was a giant "fuck you" to all the draft dodgers and protestors when they'd come back to a country that spat on them.

Con held her fiercely. Then he looked toward Bobby, who had walked up behind her. "You must be the cop."

Maggie turned and saw Bobby nod and hold out his hand, which Con shook.

"Danny," Con said, turning to her brother, "you're a fucking mess. I hope they look worse."

Danny shook his head slowly and spoke, his speech nasal from his probably broken nose. "Nah. Three of them, only one of me."

"Come on in," Con said, opening the door to his cabin. He let the three of them enter first, and Maggie watched as he scanned the woods warily before shutting the door.

Once inside, she and Bobby settled on the gleaming leather couch, and Danny sat in a recliner that looked brand new. Con walked to the kitchen and returned with a bottle of Jack Daniel's and a two-liter of Coke. He went back to the kitchen, which was really not much more than a cooking area off the main room of the cabin, and came back with four glasses.

"You still not drinking?" he asked Maggie as he sat down in a worn leather recliner, clearly the only chair he ever used.

"Yeah."

Con poured her a soda. He looked at Bobby. "You?"

"Coke is fine."

Con handed Danny a tall glass of Jack Daniel's without asking, and then poured himself one.

"Your father's over there, on the fireplace. Here's to the greatest man I ever knew. A hero."

Maggie, Danny and Bobby all looked over at the fireplace where a brass box, an urn, sat on the mantel. Maggie stared at it, her eyes burning, grateful for Bobby's hand resting on her thigh, or she probably would have traded up to a J.D.

Maggie sipped her drink and thought back to when she'd seen with her own eyes what Con was made of, why her father had trusted him as he'd trusted no one else outside his family.

"What can I get you?" Maggie balanced her small, round cocktail tray on her hip and looked down at the two men who'd wandered into the Twilight. It was late, and their eyes were already bloodshot. She didn't like the look of them. The one guy was wearing a leather jacket with metal studs along the collar. The other was clearly oblivious to the January windchill and wore a black T-shirt, his arms chapped and raw-looking, as if he'd been walking outside a while. She didn't recognize them. Neither did her brother, she gathered, as she saw Danny checking them out from behind the bar. The Twilight wasn't a place you went to unless you were known, at least back then.

"I'll have a double shot of Wild Turkey," the one with the leather jacket said. He had a gold tooth that flashed in his mouth when he spoke, and the letters K-I-L-L were etched in prison-tattoo ink across the knuckles of his left hand.

"Me, too," said the other one, sniffling and twitching.

Maggie strode over to the bar.

"Two Wild Turkeys. Double shots."

Danny reached for the bottle, pulled down two glasses and muttered under his breath, "Seen those two before?"

"No. Could be Westies. Could just be punks. Either way, they're trouble."

Her brother nodded. Both of them had worked the Twilight since they could stand on a box and reach the register. They knew trouble by what it ordered, how it sat, how it moved.

Danny set the drinks on Maggie's cocktail round. "I'm watching." He jerked his head toward the end of the bar. "So's Con."

Con was nursing a Jack Daniel's, looking, to others, like a vet slumped in a bar stool, but Maggie knew absolutely nothing escaped his eye. She relaxed a bit, returned to the two strangers and set their drinks down on the wooden table.

"That'll be twenty-two dollars."

"How much more for a piece of ass?" The one with the leather jacket leered at her and tried to pull her on his lap.

Maggie managed to wriggle out of his grasp and said, calmly, "The guy behind the bar is my brother. I don't think you want to try anything, asshole."

The other punk sniffed and let out an amused chuckle. "He don't look like much." With that, he reached out a hand and pinched her right breast so roughly that tears came to her eyes.

Maggie's reaction was instantaneous. She slapped him hard across the face, even as she bent over and clutched her breast.

Con was at the table in the time it took for the prick who'd pinched her to try again.

"What do you want?" the one in the T-shirt asked.

"Touch her again and you won't be walking out of this bar in one piece."

The one in the leather jacket sneered. "Says who? An old man?"

His friend snorted a laugh.

"I'll tell you one more time. If you want to get out of here in one piece, leave your drinks on the table, tip the lady and get lost."

Maggie stood next to Con, certain these two assholes couldn't be stupid enough to face down Con, with his army jacket, its old bloodstains dark and foreboding, and those eyes of his, nearly black and always cold, like a snake's.

But the one with the *K-I-L-L* tattoo and the leather jacket decided to push it. He reached out a hand and ran it up her thigh to her crotch and gave a squeeze.

With one swift motion, Con pulled a huge blade from his belt and slammed it straight through the jerk's other hand, which was resting on the wooden table, effectively staking him there.

The creep howled like a wild animal. His friend backed his chair up, but didn't retaliate, because by now, Danny had approached with a baseball bat.

Con said icily, "I want my knife back," and pulled it from the guy's hand, as blood seeped across the table and dripped on the floor. Con wiped the knife on his jacket, a fresh stain added to old ones, and put it away, and the other man held his hand to his chest, still whimpering.

"If I ever see you again, I'll take a permanent souvenir," Con said. "The door's that way."

Both men hightailed it out of there. Con didn't say a word to Maggie and just returned to his drink as if nothing had happened. Maggie and Danny didn't speak of the event to their father when he came back from whatever it was he was doing over in Nigeria. They didn't speak of it to each other. They just knew that was Con. He was the family pit bull.

"Do you know how he died?" Maggie finally asked after Con and Danny each had a second drink. Con had also given Danny two painkillers, and Danny's eyes now had that glazed look, so Maggie knew he was more comfortable.

Con shook his head as he looked over at the urn. The cabin wasn't primitive. It was equipped with lots of electronic gadgets and two plasma-screen televisions—one in the loft where Con slept and one in the great room where the four of them sat. The fireplace was immense, and when a blaze roared, it was enough to heat the place, although Con had a wood-burning stove in the loft. The log-beam walls were covered in old photos, mostly of Con and Maggie's father and of Maggie and Danny throughout their lives. Two book-shelves were lined with books, no novels, only volumes on philosophy, Buddhism, Lao-tzu.

"I don't know how he died. The urn arrived by FedEx of all fucking things. With a letter from a lawyer, a real lawyer, I checked, saying I was named executor and I was assigned the ashes."

"And?"

"And nothing. I'm just absorbing all this myself. Your father always said if he turned up dead, it would be because of them."

"Who's them?" Bobby asked, squinting.

Con said nothing. His eyes didn't even register that Bobby had spoken.

Danny pointed at Bobby. "Look, Con, he's with her. We can trust him."

"I don't know," Con said.

"I'll go outside if you want to talk with them alone," Bobby offered.

"No, stay." Maggie grabbed his hand.

"All right," Con finally said, his shaved head and dark eyes making him look reptilian. "It's the CIA. And these two—" he motioned to Maggie and Danny "—are in big fucking trouble."

Chapter Nine

Saigon, April 26, 1975

Saigon was falling.

Jimmy Malone felt panic rise in the form of acid in his throat. He swallowed hard, putting the fear in its place, the way he'd taught himself to do long ago. Always, when he put the panic in its own prison in his chest, there came a cold calm.

The streets were teeming with people, a cacophony of voices and heat, beeping horns, bicycle bells, screams and the occasional sound of gunfire, rat-a-tatting in the distance. Over a bullhorn, someone was shouting in Vietnamese. He heard Laotian, Vietnamese, French, English, and bastardized Mandarin tongues clucking and shouting. He had learned, over time, to distinguish between the foreign languages he barely understood. He knew Vietnamese people couldn't make the *th* sound and their language sounded harsh to him, the way the voices rose and fell, punctuated with urgency as tongues clicked against teeth.

He pushed past the USO club, turned a corner and walked a couple more blocks before he arrived at the brothel and pushed his way in the door, looking for Con. He spied Con's best girl and made his way to her.

"Seen him today?"

She shook her head.

"If you see him, tell him I'm looking for him, that I'm making my way to the embassy. American embassy. Okay?"

She nodded, a quiver in her lip. "What become of us?"

"Who?"

"Me." She looked around at the room full of Vietnamese women dressed in cheap lingerie. "The girls. Vietnam."

Jimmy shrugged. "Vietnam has outlived every occupying government long before we got here. It'll survive. So will you."

He hadn't the time to worry about anyone else. He turned and forced his way out into the streets, where crowds jostled and cyclists pressed the little bells on their handlebars, the tinkling joy of bells mocking the chaos and tragedy on the streets. Jimmy was grateful he was a head and a half taller than the populace. He maneuvered, looking for openings in the crowd, pushing his way to his destination.

Turning down a side street, he found a plain door, opened it and took the stairs two and three at a time to the top floor where he kept a sparsely furnished apartment. He unlocked the door and felt a rush of relief when he saw Mai was there.

He ran to her and kissed her hard, feeling his pulse pound. He was desperate to get her out.

"Listen to me," he said, gripping her arms tightly, as if somehow that would convey his strength into her. "You've got to get on a chopper today. Con and I have a buddy, and we're getting you in the gate, and Hank will see that you get out."

"But what about you?" Her voice was soft. He had taught her English. She had helped him improve his Vietnamese.

"I'll come stateside when I can. When you get to the U.S., someone will come get you. I've made arrangements. Con and I. You'll go to Boston, to my brother's, but just for a short time. Then I'll get you down to New York. Mai, I promise you, I'm getting you to America."

"And Tam?"

Jimmy nodded, reluctantly. Saigon was falling, as if the entire world were caving in and collapsing, and Mai needed to get this one baby out of there. Which meant Jimmy had to, because if he didn't, Mai wouldn't leave, and the way things had been going, he knew that would be a death sentence for her. He prayed Con was successful, buying off the man who ran the orphanage, bribing guys in the embassy. Vietnamese officials. A Vietnamese marriage certificate, that not a few months before cost you twenty bucks, now cost two grand. It was only money, Jimmy told himself.

"I'm workin' on it."

"My baby sister."

Jimmy sighed. "Come on. We've got to go."

Mai had packed only a single bag, like he'd told her, which she slung over her neck and across her body. She was wearing an American undershirt beneath the shirt and skirt she wore, and wrapped against her body were stacks of hundreds.

"I'm..." She searched for the word. Eventually, she took Jimmy's hand and pressed it to her forehead.

He caressed her face. "Sweating. I know. The money is

going to make you feel hotter. But trust me, if you get in any kind of trouble you buy your way out, Mai. It's only money. *Buy* your way out. You got me? Spend every cent if you have to."

She nodded. Jimmy brushed a strand of hair from her face, tracing her high cheekbones with his index finger. Around her neck, she wore his dog tags. He told her they would bring her luck. He also wanted everyone to know she was his, not as a piece of property so much as a warning. You fuck with this girl, you fuck with Jimmy Malone. He would hunt down and kill anyone who harmed her—in country or not.

Taking her hand, he took one last look around the apartment where they'd made love and shut out the war so many times. The two of them exited the door, and he locked it. They hurried down the narrow hallway and the still-narrower staircase, the scent of cabbage in the air, and then out into the streets. Jimmy gripped her hand tighter, knowing if they got separated now, he'd lose her forever. He felt like a drowning man holding on to a life jacket.

Arms wrapped around her, clutching her, he half dragged, half pulled her to the gates of the embassy and scanned the crowd for Con. Looking through the fence, he spied his contact. Hank was hard to miss with his flaming orange hair and pale skin freckled like a Dalmatian. Jimmy glanced at his watch. In ten minutes, as planned, Hank came to the wrought-iron gates, gave Jimmy a nod, and Mai was let through, lifted high and over the top of the gate as other women and children and men screamed for mercy, screamed to be let in, too. Jimmy didn't even have time to kiss her goodbye. He could only use his wide back and strong arms to form a barricade between her and others as she was let in. He felt hands clawing at him, scratching him.

"Tam!" she called over her shoulder, looking in Jimmy's eyes.

"She'll be here," Jimmy shouted back. He watched as Hank ushered her to a waiting helicopter. Jimmy thought it was the most expensive helicopter ride in the history of aviation.

After the copter took off, he turned from the embassy and walked through the pandemonium in the streets, hoping to see Con. His best friend was nowhere in sight. Jimmy tried not to worry. It was a tall order, trying to get a woman and a toddler out of Vietnam. An impossible order. But everything in Vietnam had a price, and Jimmy had told Con that whatever the price, Tam had to get to America. Jimmy would have preferred Tam and Mai to leave together, but Tam's papers were late, and in the chaos, there was no time. Now, she would be smuggled out as an orphan. Jimmy went to his favorite bar to wait.

The sun was starting to hang low in the sky when Jimmy heard Con over the crowd. "Malone! Malone!"

Jimmy turned his head in the direction of his friend's voice and saw him carrying little Tam. She was calm, smiling, oblivious to the price paid for her release, oblivious to the masses around her that might soon be dead without passage to America.

Con reached Jimmy. He wore a thick handlebar mustache and had a sleepy, stoner look that belied how deadly he could be if crossed.

"Got her," he said beaming, tousling her wild black hair with its endlessly silly cowlicks.

"Thank fuckin' God." The two comrades stood in the midst of chaos and tickled Tam under her chin, letting her wrap her chubby fists around their fingers.

Jimmy lowered his head and nuzzled her. "Be safe, little one." She pulled on his hair and giggled.

Con asked him, "Mai?"

Jimmy nodded. They'd flown enough missions, been through enough terror in the jungles together to no longer need many words to communicate.

Jimmy and Con made their way toward the airport, which was pockmarked with small craters from explosions. Busloads of orphans waited on the tarmac. Jimmy looked for his contact and spotted a bearded young orphanage worker. The contact came over to Jimmy.

"Godspeed, Tam," Jimmy whispered under his breath.

He and Con stood, like little boys, faces pressed against the fences surrounding the tarmac, until Tam was a speck in the distance. Now, it was up to all of the people Jimmy had bought off to bring both Mai and Tam to the place he called home.

He and Con, wordlessly, in tandem, turned from the fence and melted into the crowds and the street. Out of habit, Jimmy made the sign of the cross. He hadn't been to a church since high school. Mai had kept a shrine to Buddha in their apartment. Whatever god and demons ruled the strange world of rivers and rice paddies, Jimmy prayed he would allow the safe passage of the woman and the little girl.

Chapter Ten

Maggie's eyes kept glancing at the urn. How could a man as powerful, fearless and dangerous as her father be reduced to ash?

"Con?" she asked. "Did they put rice and money in...you know, when they cremated him?"

"That was important to him," Danny said.

Con nodded. "Actually, this lawyer said he'd given instructions for that."

"So who is this lawyer? How did Dad end up contacting him and not us? We're next of kin," Maggie asked.

Con sighed. Maggie waited patiently. Con wasn't someone you rushed. He looked down into his glass.

"They put rice and money in."

Maggie closed her eyes and waited. No one said anything, and she was aware of the tick-tick-tick of the clock on the mantel. The clock that sat next to her father.

"Look," Con finally said, "the lawyer was someone your father and I knew in country. He and your dad kept in touch all these years. He was someone we both trusted. And he was helping your dad…with certain investigations."

Maggie looked over at Danny, then at Con. "Who did this to Danny? Do you know what they want? Do you even know who they are? If you do, Con, we have to know."

Again she was aware of the clock, as if it were taunting her.

"If I were you," Con said, "I'd sell the bar and go someplace far away."

"Didn't my father try that?" Maggie said. "And didn't he end up on your mantel over there?"

Bobby leaned forward. "We can go to the FBI. Whatever this is, there have to be people who can protect Maggie. Protect Danny."

Con shook his head and smiled derisively at Bobby. "You poor, dumb fuck. You don't get it. The people you think can protect these two are the people who want to kill them."

"I don't understand," Bobby said.

"What I'm saying is they need to live like their old man and me. One eye over their shoulder at all times."

Danny leaned his head to one side and glanced at Con through glazed eyes. "Con, shit…man, that's fine. We live like that. We booby-trap our fucking lives, but what the hell are we running from?"

"I can only tell you what I know."

"Fine. We'll take whatever scraps you can give us, Con," Danny said, "but just tell us."

Con stood up wordlessly and crossed the wide-plank floor of the cabin, his work boots clomping on the wood as he walked. He climbed up the ladder to the loft, and Maggie could hear him opening drawers and doors, sighing. He was gone about fifteen minutes. When he returned, he was stone-faced and clenching his jaw.

"Here." He handed Maggie two photos and then started pacing. Maggie looked down. One was a photograph of her parents in Vietnam. Her father was wearing his army pants and a white T-shirt, a pack of cigarettes rolled in the sleeve; her mother was a beautiful girl with a broken smile. She looked like she was very much in love with the soldier standing next to her, but just as Maggie remembered her, there was sadness to her smile. Maggie's father had his arm around her shoulders. A hut was in the background. The sky was clear, but the colors were like photos from the 1960s, muted with the flattest of greens and blues. Maggie smiled at seeing her parents so young, in a place she'd only heard of. She touched the picture of her mother, almost like a talisman, passing her index finger over the top of her face. She handed Bobby the picture.

"She was beautiful," he whispered before passing the photo to Danny. Her brother looked at the photo briefly and then looked away. He cleared his throat.

The next photo was of her father and a baby. "Who's this?"

"Tam," Con said.

"Tam," Maggie repeated. She'd heard the name only once before.

Maggie heard them fighting. Not fighting so much as talking passionately. They never fought. Not ever. They never even said snide things to each other or hinted at anger. Never a harsh word. No edges of sarcasm. When she got older, Maggie wondered sometimes if she had imagined how much they'd loved each other, if she had somehow idealized her parents, but she knew she remembered them correctly. Theirs was an intense, once-in-a-lifetime love. But this night, they were whispering loudly. Maggie heard her mother crying.

Maggie climbed out of bed, clutching her Strawberry Shortcake doll, and crept to the door, which was cracked open just a bit. Her mother was kneeling on the red silk pillow in front of the Buddha altar, and she had her face buried in her hands, crying. Incense burned, the scent of jasmine reaching Maggie's nostrils.

"Don't cry, Mai. Please," her father urged as he touched her shoulder.

Her mother, with a vehemence Maggie didn't know she possessed, looked up at him with fury and grief. "I must cry."

He knelt down next to her. First, out of deference to her, he bowed to Buddha as she had taught them all. Then he reached out and brushed her hair off her face, tilting her head toward him so he could see her eyes.

"I made a promise to you, Mai. I will find her. I've never given up. Not for a day, a minute. In country…here…Laos. I have never stopped looking."

"One baby. One baby…how can she be so hard to find?"

"I will find her. Whatever it takes."

Maggie's mother bowed her head and said the name. "Tam."

"Yes, Tam." He put his forehead to hers.

"Means *heart*."

"Hmm?"

"Tam. It means *heart*." She took her husband's hand and placed it on her left breast. "She is my heart."

Maggie's father lifted his head and nodded. Then her mother pulled out the dog tags she always wore hidden beneath her shirt, and let them fall between her breasts, around her neck. She never took them off. His dog tags. She lifted one.

"You gave me these. Said I was your girl."

"You are my girl."

"Then get me my heart back. Please." Her voice was pleading, desperate.

Maggie heard her father groan. It was an anguished cry she only heard one other time, later, when her mother's body was found.

He grabbed Maggie's mother, pulled her close to his chest and kissed her fiercely on the mouth. From her vantage point, Maggie felt shame, as if she shouldn't be seeing this raw scene between them. She sneaked back to bed and fell asleep with the word *Tam* on her lips.

Heart.

"Tam," Maggie said. "It means heart."

"How do you know that? Did your father tell you about her?" Con asked.

Maggie shook her head. "No. I heard them one night. My mother was crying. Who is she?"

"Your sister."

"What?" Maggie's hands began to tremble and she dropped the photo.

Danny sat up. "What are you talking about?" He grabbed the photo from Maggie's lap and stared at it. Bobby leaned over to look, too.

"Half sister," Con said. "We didn't even know that until a while ago. After your mother died."

"She looks like you," Danny said and handed the photo back to Maggie.

"She does, doesn't she?" Maggie whispered.

"Half sister," Danny said. "Who's her father?"

"That…that's what your father was killed for."

Chapter Eleven

Vietnam, April 1971

Soldiers came to Mai's village. Her father wanted no part of either side. He wanted to attend to his rice paddies. He wanted the war to be over. But it was no secret that some others wanted the Americans to leave.

They came. A platoon of them. Mai was sixteen, and she was washing clothes in the stream. She peered through the grass as she heard the pop-pop-popping of guns. Her father had always told her to hide if she heard gunfire. So she did as he'd told her.

Lying flat on her back, she prayed to be unseen, invisible, in the grasses. Like a tiger, maybe. She shut her eyes. When she opened them again, two soldiers were standing over her, peering down. She stared up and prayed that perhaps they could not see her, that somehow she had turned to spirit.

They were young. One held his gun pointed down at her head. He was sweating, and he smiled at her. Mean, like he hated her. They could see her. The other, she noticed, had flung his gun around his back and was unbuckling his belt and unzipping his pants. He was on her instantly, his hand over her mouth, although she wouldn't have screamed anyway—she wouldn't have wanted her father or someone else from the village to come and be shot. He ripped her pants, tearing them. They were threadbare, and the cloth was soft.

It was painful. It was nothing like she thought it might be. It burned. She didn't look down there, but she knew she was bleeding.

He kept his hand on her mouth, and he was grunting and pounding against her. She arched her spine in resistance and tilted her neck back so she was looking at the sky and not the soldier's face.

He pushed down on her throat and said something in English she didn't understand. But she knew what he was trying to do. He wanted her to look him in the eyes.

She did. She stared at him with all the hatred she could muster. He looked down at her, and then pulled out of her and knelt back. He removed his hand from her mouth and slapped her so hard her face slammed into the mud as it snapped to the side.

She told herself to look away. They would shoot her, kill her, and it would be done. She would go to her next life. But instead he grabbed her by her long hair and forced her to look at him again. He said the same words, unintelligible to her, and he slapped her again, even harder.

The other soldier, the one with the gun aimed at her, spat on her face. Then, from over the hill, back toward the village, two helicopters swooped down. Mai heard yelling and then gunfire—not single pop, pop, pops, but the rapid-fire sound of hundreds of bullets coming in rounds from mounted machine guns.

The two soldiers turned from her and ran in the direction of the village. Mai was left, legs bloodied, face swelling, dirt in her hair and up her nose. She lay there a long time. Somehow, she could not make herself move.

The helicopters went away, and still she could not move. She heard her uncle calling for her, and yet she lay there, eyes fixed on a single rock next to her.

The sun set. Sometime after dark, her uncle and her cousin found her. They scooped her into their arms, as if she were a little girl, and they carried her to the village.

There, she learned her father was dead. So were several other men, one woman, and little Bao, a baby boy, as well as some of their pigs and a few chickens. Two homes were completely burned, their grasses no match for the firepower of the Americans.

Her mother asked Mai what had happened. Months later, when Mai's belly grew round, she asked her again. Mai said she remembered nothing. But that wasn't true.

No, it wasn't true at all. She remembered the way one soldier had spat on her, and then how a bit of spittle had gathered in the corner of his mouth. She remembered how badly it had stung when the other had been inside her. She remembered the feel of dirt on her cheek, gritty and painful. She remembered, when the soldier had been on her, how his sharp stubble had chafed her. Her father had not grown facial hair. His face had never hurt her when he'd bent to pick her up.

But above all, she remembered the cold, lifeless eyes of the evil spirit who'd raped her. He'd had the body of a man but the dead eyes of something from another world of angry spirits. And she remembered that he'd been burned. On his neck. It had clearly healed somewhat, but his neck still looked raw and red, and raised, the way burns sometimes buckled. The burn had spread up his neck from beneath the collar of his army uniform.

The vision of that burn and the soldier's dead eyes would be a part of Mai forever. So would Tam.

Though Mai's village felt great shame over Mai's condition, Mai believed Tam was her heart. She believed that as the evil man had entered her, Buddha had somehow made sure that a good spirit had made a baby from just her heart. Not the man. Just her, Mai, and her heart.

Chapter Twelve

Danny struggled to focus in the haze of pain, drugs and Jack Daniel's. When Con finished telling them about Tam, Danny wanted to cry. It hurt him to think that his mother, who was the gentlest human being he'd ever known, had been so brutalized.

But now that he knew about Tam, some things suddenly made sense. Like the way his mother had been so superstitious. He knew she was a Buddhist, their father a Christmas-Easter Catholic, but she'd taken both their religions and had used every spirit tool at her disposal to keep Danny and Maggie safe. He used to think her paranoia was a result of living in Hell's Kitchen, that she was wary of the Westies and the brutality of the neighborhood. But now he had to assume it was the specter of Tam taking residence in that apartment with them.

His mother used to bless them with holy water, dousing their foreheads. Danny remembered their father chiding her playfully. "A little sign of the cross will do it, Mai." But she would cup one hand and pour holy water from a jar into it and then wipe it on her children's hair and foreheads. She used to go to church for morning mass—maybe a handful of penitent Catholics showed up for mass each day. She would bring jelly jars, and when the priest was busy, she would scoop up full jars of the water, convinced it had special powers.

Danny remembered once going to St. Patrick's Cathedral with her. They'd walked the perimeter, and the visit had taken hours. He and Maggie knew better than to whine about church or Buddha, but he remembered feeling frustrated. Mai insisted they kneel and light a candle at every altar in the church. Mai had taken a roll of bills from the safe in the back office of the Twilight, and she slipped singles into the small iron boxes for the poor at every altar. They lit candles in front of the Virgin Mary and a dozen or more marble saints in alcoves off the main part of the church. Every footstep echoed, and they could hear the rites of mass being conducted.

On the way out of the cathedral, there was a small religious shop. Mai took Danny by one hand and Maggie by the other, then entered the little shop and looked at the hundreds of religious medals and crucifixes and tiny statues.

Peeling off twenties from her Twilight bankroll, Mai bought thirty or more religious medallions.

"What do you need all of them for?" Maggie asked her.

"Covering bases," she said.

When they got back to Hell's Kitchen, before their father came up from the bar for dinner, Mai went through the entire apartment hiding the medals. After that, it hadn't been uncommon for Danny or Maggie to lie down on the couch and stick their hand in the cushion and find a St. Jude medal, or to water a plant and find a hidden St. Patrick in the dirt.

"I can't imagine my mother going through that," Maggie said, echoing Danny's thoughts.

Con nodded.

"So what became of Tam?" Bobby asked.

Con said, "Jimmy and I got Mai out on a helicopter from the U.S. Embassy. We had a connection inside, and Jimmy had been stockpiling money for a while. We both had. And there was a lot. He spent most of it getting the two of them out of there. In the commotion as Saigon was falling, your dad had stashed Tam in an orphanage temporarily while he secured papers for her and your mother. It was an insane time. They were originally supposed to leave together—your mother and Tam. But…Tam went on a different helicopter during Operation Babylift. At that time, we all thought she was your mother's baby sister. She never told us Tam was her daughter. We didn't know. I swear to God we didn't know."

"What happened when they got here?" Maggie asked.

"More confusion. At first, we thought…" Con was silent for a minute or two, looking down at his forearm where a dragon tattoo from Vietnam curled around, identical to one on Jimmy's forearm. Finally, he looked up at them again. "You know, your mother didn't tell us everything. We thought Tam was lost in red tape. We didn't know. We didn't know until much later."

"Know what?" Danny demanded.

Con paced some more. Then he sat down. Then he stood again. Danny had known Con a long time. His memories of childhood were fluid, his mother and father and Maggie and Con and Jesus and Buddha and Hell's Kitchen wrapped in one long seamless fabric. And never, in all those memories, had Con ever been scared. Paranoid, maybe, but never scared.

"She had something. She had filmed something." He looked at Danny and Maggie. "Remember when Kennedy was shot? The film? The grassy knoll, the magic bullet?"

Danny just stared, confused.

"You unlucky fucking bastards. In Vietnam, your mother took her own fucking Zapruder film. An eight-millimeter nightmare that will kill us all if we're not careful."

Chapter Thirteen

Vietnam, July 1972

Mai Hanh loved Tam, Jimmy Malone, Buddha and her camera. In that order.

First, Jimmy had bought her a little Kodak camera. He'd taught her how to load the film, and then he would get it developed in Saigon. She loved everything about her camera. She loved looking through the lens and the clickety-click sound it made when she wound the film through. But the most satisfying part was getting the pictures back. Jimmy was so good to her. He would never open the pictures without her. He would wait until they were together, sometimes with Tam on her lap, and they would look through them and laugh.

Her favorite picture ever was of Jimmy holding Tam. The baby was smiling, and Jimmy had his face leaned down close to hers and was kissing her cheek. Sometimes Mai pretended that Tam was Jimmy's. But the rest of the time, she told herself Tam was born from a single seed in Mai's heart.

One day, Jimmy showed up with a different kind of camera.

"What this?" she asked him.

"It takes moving pictures."

When she didn't understand, he tried explaining over and over again until finally she just believed what he said about his magic camera. It would take pictures and hold them inside like they were alive until she could make them move outside. It made as much sense as a magic seed in her heart and the miracle of Tam.

They took moving pictures. Then Jimmy took a wheel of film from inside the camera. Weeks later, he arrived with a white bedsheet and a magic light-box. It had two round wheels and when Jimmy was through, they had threaded the film through the magic box and watched, at night, as Tam and Jimmy and Mai appeared, moving and alive, on the bedsheet.

Mai started to cry.

"Oh, baby, don't cry." He stopped the machine. "Look. See…I'm here and you're here and Tam's here. Isn't it cool, baby? Like magic. Don't be afraid."

But Mai wasn't afraid. She was in love with the camera. She stood and went over to the bedsheet and asked him to turn on the magic box again. She touched the sheet and watched as the baby appeared on her palm. Her heart fluttered. It was a miracle. After that, the order was the same. Tam, Jimmy Malone, Buddha and her camera. But this camera, the one with the moving pictures, was a very close fourth behind Buddha.

Her village was quiet now. Almost as if it had died. People had left for Saigon, and she and Tam and her mother were going to leave, too. Jimmy was finalizing arrangements. Her mother cluck-clucked. The American soldier wouldn't stay if he knew about Tam. Mai didn't believe her mother, but she kept her secret. She said Tam was her sister. And she hid her camera in the special hiding spot in the ground that Jimmy and his friends had built for her. She knew her neighbor Tran was jealous of her magic camera, and she didn't want anything to happen to it. Jimmy made her hide American dollars inside her shoes, too. The war was a crazy time, and it seemed like it was always about hiding things and secrets.

One night, an explosion rocked the fields. Mai heard gunfire, so she grabbed Tam and woke her mother, and ran from their hut to the hiding place. As she was running with Tam in her arms, she felt heat on her face, and when she looked to her left, she saw the world on fire. They rushed through the brush with no shoes on, yet she didn't even feel the dirt beneath her. There was no time. They pushed the reeds aside and squeezed, the three of them, into the hole. Tam was crying, and Mai rocked her as best she could in the black space of the hole, until, miraculously, the baby fell asleep. Mai leaned her cheek against the baby's soft skin and tried to remain hopeful.

Mai could hear her mother breathing. Her mother was getting very old. She had lost a husband and a son to the war, and her only other brother was missing. Her sister was with the Frenchman. *Tante* sent money, but Mai knew her mother disapproved. Just as she disapproved of Tam. The fact that Mai had given birth to a girl, who could not help take care of Mai when she was old, was a sign.

Mai pulled the reeds over their hiding spot. It was hot, and dirt settled on the nape of her neck. She imagined bugs crawling all around her, and her skin betrayed her by getting an itching, tingling feeling as if a million tiny legs were creeping across her body.

Her arms were tired, and she wordlessly handed Tam to her mother. She heard screaming, and then she thought of the camera. She would show Jimmy what happened. She would show him, as long as they survived this night.

She felt around in the darkness and her fingers touched the cloth in which the camera was wrapped. She took the camera out and held it up to her eye. She used it to peer out, but all she could see was grass. Using her fingers, she parted the tangled shoots slightly. Against the black sky, she filmed explosions and screaming, and she filmed silhouettes of soldiers gunning down people she had known her whole life, but it was far away and it was as if she were filming just shadows and fire. It didn't seem real, like it was all inside the magic box. She stopped the camera and instead just leaned against her mother and Tam, hoping and praying that they would remain undiscovered.

The screaming lasted all night, until, by morning, there were no more screams. Mai heard helicopters. She peered out, and not more than fifteen yards away, she could see a soldier. Tam was still sleeping, as was her mother. Mai wriggled a tiny bit and, though her arms were numb from not moving all night, she managed to hoist the camera to her eye and film. Another soldier walked over to the first soldier, and they spat on a dead body. They said some things in English. And then the first soldier turned.

Mai's heart stopped. Years later, she was convinced she'd died for a moment. For when the soldier turned, Mai saw that he was burned on his neck. It was him. She filmed as he took a knife and sliced an ear off the old man, Thich, who was dead on the ground. The burned man, the one who was an evil spirit, laughed. Then they walked toward the landing helicopters and the soldiers climbed in, leaving nothing, not a single water buffalo or pig or person, alive in her village. Except for Tam, Mai and her mother. In the hiding spot. Except for the people alive in spirit inside her magic box.

Chapter Fourteen

Bobby Gonzalez knew a bunch of cops who had served tours in Vietnam. Some were coming up on retirement. They shared one thing in common. None of them liked to talk about what had happened over there.

"So Maggie's mother filmed a village massacre."

Con nodded.

"I mean, a lot of crazy shit went on in that war. It doesn't sound to me like, you know, this would be enough of a reason to kill people. Not now. Not after all this time."

Con finally flopped into his chair. He poured himself a bourbon and drank it fast and without blinking. "Yeah. Except Mai hit the fucking trifecta."

"What do you mean?" Danny asked.

Con ran his hands over his face. He hadn't shaved, and though Bobby didn't know him, he noticed the shadows, the circles, underneath his eyes. He guessed they weren't always there. "Mai talked a lot about karma, right?"

Bobby looked at Maggie and then her brother. They both nodded.

"Well," Con continued, "I don't know what the hell she did in her last life, because she brought a fucking hailstorm of shit down on herself in this one."

"I can't protect Maggie if I don't know what it is I'm protecting her from," Bobby said. His headache was pounding now.

"You know," Con said, "there are explosives underneath my front steps. All I have to do is press a button and anyone on my porch will turn into little pieces of flesh hanging on the tree branches."

Bobby stared at Maggie's uncle. For not the first time, he wondered what the hell kind of family this was. "Uh-huh," he said cautiously. "And?"

"And I mean that whatever department-issued revolver you got isn't protection. I mean you need shit like C-4. The only reason he's alive—" Con jerked his head toward Danny "—and not like their old man in the urn, is they don't have the film yet, and obviously Jimmy didn't give it up. Not that I'd expect him to. After Vietnam, after the shit we saw, torture ain't that fucking scary."

Bobby swallowed hard. When he was a kid, when he was a punk, he'd mugged someone once. He'd been in more than his share of bar fights, and he'd never backed down, not even when the other guy was a six-foot-two meth-head with an attitude over the girl Bobby was with at the time.

"Okay, I'll bite, Con," Bobby said, tired of the riddles and wanting a straight answer. "Who's on the film?"

"You really want to know?"

Bobby nodded. So did Maggie and Danny.

"Once you know, there's no going back."

Bobby whispered, "I don't scare as easy as you think I do."

"Fine." Con stood up and crossed the room, his boots clomping on the wood again. He went up into the loft. Bobby glanced at Maggie and Danny. Neither appeared to think Con's way of either defending his house or guarding their family secrets was unusual.

He came back down with a copy of *Time* magazine. "Here."

He laid the magazine on the table.

Maggie looked at Con. "I don't get it."

But Bobby did. He forgot all that bullshit about not scaring easy. Suddenly blown-up bits of flesh on trees and C-4 made sense. He looked at Con desperately, willing the tough old soldier to tell him it wasn't what he thought it was.

Con stabbed an index finger at the cover. "Him."

"What?" Maggie asked again.

"Him. That's the fucker who torched the village. And that's Tam's father."

Maggie went pale. Danny groaned.

"How do you know?" Bobby asked.

"For that, you have to learn the rest of the story, just like Jimmy and I did. We learned it in pieces over thirty years. But on my life, he's the bastard. And the film proves at least part of that."

"So where's the film, Con?" Danny asked.

"Atlantic City."

"Shit," said Danny.

"The film is with Hop."

Bobby didn't know what that meant. What he did know was Maggie's mother's shit storm was raining hard on them. Staring up at them from the coffee table was the face of Senator John S. Calhoun III, beneath a headline that read At Last, Will a Real Hero Run for the White House?

Chapter Fifteen

New Jersey Shore, August 1986

It was late at night and Maggie and Danny sat on the sidewalk outside Asbury Park's Angel Tavern counting motorcycles. Seventeen. All shiny, all Harleys. Maggie wondered if only Harleys were allowed to park there, and she would have asked Danny what he thought, but she was afraid he'd call her stupid. Uncle Con had told her since she could remember that Harleys were the only bikes that mattered. Anything else was a "Jap" bike, whatever that meant.

A fawn-colored pit bull on a chain was tied to a lamppost. It would strain the chain, trying to get closer to Maggie, who cooed to it. "Hello, boy," she whispered softly. "Hello, boy."

"Don't talk to that dog," Danny told her.

"I want a puppy."

Danny rolled his eyes. "Yeah, but that dog will eat you. So don't talk to it."

Maggie looked the dog in the eyes. "You wouldn't eat me, would you, boy?"

The pit bull growled.

Maggie leaned her elbows on her knees. "When are they coming out?" she whined.

Danny shrugged and craned his neck, looking into the Angel. A giant set of wings were painted on the front window of the place, and loud rock music assaulted their ears. The front door was open and a bouncer sat on a tall stool outside on the sidewalk.

Maggie sighed. Whenever Uncle Con showed up, it usually meant strange midnight runs. Before their mother had died, they would have stayed at home, but now, more often than not, they were dragged along for the ride. Her father said he felt better knowing they were near him. Tonight they were seeing Hop.

Hop frightened Maggie. For one thing, he liked to play with knives. He wore one—a huge blade as big as a carving knife—strapped to his calf. He liked to take it out and hurl it at the wall when he was mad. And unlike Uncle Con, who would get down on the floor and give her a pony ride or would read her *The Velveteen Rabbit,* Hop despised children. He even said so right in front of them. Well, that wasn't true exactly. He hated half-breeds and didn't understand how their father could have married "one of the enemy."

Maggie didn't understand why her father put up with Hop. One time, after Hop had said something about their mother, their father had pulled out a gun and aimed it right at Hop's head. After that, Hop didn't say much about half-breeds. Still, their dad told her and Danny that only two other men in the world, besides himself, would never "give it up," whatever *it* was, Maggie had no idea.

"Hop would die before he'd give up the dead," her father had once told her. She didn't understand, but Hop had the same tattoo as Con and her father, and after their mother had died, he was a little nicer to her and Danny. He even gave her a tiny blue glass eyeball, like a marble, suspended from a gold pin.

"To ward off the evil eye," he had said to her. "Wear it on your undershirt." She had pinned it, yet another way of covering her bases.

The night wore on. Maggie and Danny watched the people walking down the street. Motorcycle boots and tattoos, tiny bikini tops on the women—and more tattoos, red bandannas hanging from the backs of Levi's pockets or wrapped around shaved heads. Silver chains dangled from wallets to belt loops. From her vantage point on the curb, Maggie saw knives strapped to calves or tucked into pockets, the shape of a switchblade perfectly outlined through tight jeans. Sometimes the bulge of the knife was gone, leaving just the faded pale blue outline of the knife's shape, the denim worn and frayed by always storing the same item in the pocket.

Maggie knew how to be invisible. For all the people walking by, no one noticed her and Danny. Maggie knew never to look as if they needed help, as if they wanted to talk. It was best to keep to themselves, to each other, Daddy, Uncle Con. Maggie carried a tiny porcelain good fortune kitty in her pocket, its paw raised up. Sometimes she talked to the kitty—the closest she and Danny would get to a pet.

Around midnight, Con and her father finally emerged. Her father scooped her up. "Are you tired, bright eyes?"

"Nope," Maggie said as she stifled a yawn.

"Will you take us for clams now?" Danny asked. "You promised."

Her father looked at Con. "Can you believe this kid? Swallows raw clams whole like a real man." He play-punched Danny in the arm. The four of them walked two doors down to an open-air raw bar. They ordered two dozen cherrystones, and while the man shucked them, his hands moving fast as he deftly sliced them open, Con, Danny and their father sat making a concoction of Tabasco sauce, ketchup, horseradish and fresh lemon. The hotter the better.

Maggie ate a clam without sauce, just to be part of the group, but Con, her father and Danny devoured them, one after the other, slurping the clam's saltiness, tears streaming down their faces from the Tabasco.

After they ate the clams and Con and her father had three beers each, they headed back to the motel. Con carried her as they walked. She nestled her head against his neck, always liking his scent. She yawned and was comforted by the rhythm of his stride. They got to their room, and Maggie changed into her pajamas and brushed her teeth. Her father helped Danny get ready for bed, and Con tucked her into the pull-out cot. His mustache tickled her cheek as he kissed her good-night, and she fell asleep as soon as her head hit the pillow.

The next day was sunny and, as a reward for being invisible on the sidewalk, they were going to Atlantic City. They were going to walk on the boardwalk and eat taffy.

Maggie dressed in her bathing suit and shorts. She had to wear sneakers and socks because they were taking the mo-

torcycles. She put on her helmet, the shiny black one with
the dragon airbrushed on the side, and Danny put on his. She
rode with their father, and Danny rode with Con. She loved
riding. She had learned how to lean the way her father
leaned, melting into him. She also liked how people looked
at them. If they passed a car with kids in it, the kids would
point. She knew they were cool. She knew it from how people looked at her father and Con. As if they were afraid of
them. Not bad afraid, just an afraid that let them walk a
straight path and no one ever got in their way.

When they reached Atlantic City, they parked the bikes
and then walked the wooden boardwalk. She and Danny
were in their bathing suits, and she twirled in the sun and
the salty, slightly fishy air. Con wore his usual outfit of army
fatigues, motorcycle boots and muscle T-shirt. Her father
wore a muscle T-shirt, leather jacket and jeans.

At the candy store, Con bought Maggie a box of saltwater taffy. She sat on a bench with him and picked out all the
pink ones, unwrapping them and stuffing them into her
mouth, chewing until her jaw hurt. Con ate the green ones.

"Why only green?"

He shrugged. "Good luck."

"Taffy can be good luck?"

He shrugged again.

Danny got a candy apple. Then the four of them walked
some more until they came to the sign for the diving bell.

The diving bell was basically a small submarine on a leash.
It was a sub attached to a crane that cranked it in and out of
the water. You boarded at the end of the pier and the sign
promised an Underwater Spectacle. Maggie had wanted to

go in the diving bell for as long as she could remember, but she was always chicken. After her mother had drowned, Maggie was even more afraid. What if the bell filled with water, drowning her and Danny and everyone else onboard? But she swore to herself she was going on this time, and she was going to see a mermaid. Or else.

Her father paid the admission. No one else boarded, so the four of them got the bell all to themselves. They each had their own porthole to look through.

The operator of the bell closed the door. It shut with a clang, and Maggie could hear her own heartbeat. She had changed her mind, thinking of her mother drowning in the river. She wanted to tell her father to save her, but he was talking with Con, and she knew she had to be brave. He was proud of her when she was brave, like at her mother's funeral, when she hadn't cried in front of other people—only when it was her and Danny and her father and Con alone.

She tried to breathe. Slowly, as if inch by inch, the bell was lowered. At first the porthole was just covered in droplets of water, then it was halfway underwater, waves like little ripples, then the bell was fully submerged.

Maggie looked through the porthole. She squinted. But the waters of Atlantic City were murky, nothing like what she'd imagined. Each wave stirred up the ocean's floor, which sent up a cloud of tiny particles, like a tornado of sand. There was nothing to see. No mermaids. No underwater spectacle. Nothing.

Maggie turned around. The fact that there was nothing to see didn't stop Danny and Con and Daddy from looking. They peered through the portholes, their faces pressed right up against the glass. Maggie watched them. Maybe the mermaids were invisible. Or maybe the only truly interesting thing to see was each other, inside their own iron bell, safe from whatever it was that made her father booby-trap the door every night.

Chapter Sixteen

"Are you coming with us tomorrow?" Maggie asked Con.

She understood why he shook his head. He had ventured out in the world less and less over the years, fortifying his sacred woods with more firepower.

"What about Daddy?" She looked at the urn on the mantel. She and Con were whispering by the fire. Danny had crashed—Con had some OxyContin, which Danny had washed down with bourbon. Con had checked out the stitches, told Danny to take some antibiotics for two weeks, which Con had on hand, and pronounced Maggie's living-room-floor surgical skills excellent.

Bobby had fallen asleep on a sleeping bag near the couch. Maggie felt sorry for him. He was getting a crash course in secrets and war. When he slept, he always looked so beautiful, his face like a sculpture, with his high cheekbones and perfectly straight nose.

"I promised your father to scatter him at the Wall, if it ever came to that. He said he'd do the same for me. Not 'cause the war meant anything to us. I mean, I felt bad about the guys we lost, but I didn't give a fuck whether we won a rice paddy for our side or not. But I guess we both felt like the war and what we saw there made us brothers, and so when we…die, it's only right to not stick us in a hole in the ground, but to leave us there."

"Do you think Hop knows where Tam is?"

Con shrugged. "The safest way to guard a secret is to not tell a single individual all the parts of your secret. That was understood. It's the way the three of us always operated."

"Do you think Calhoun has the film?"

Con shrugged again. "I only know what that senator fucker did. I saw the film once. It was enough to remember for the rest of my life." Maggie noticed how Con's eyes perpetually squinted, their blackness eerily cold and reptilian. She wished she had known him and her father from a lifetime before, when they were less weary, less dead inside.

"I'm an orphan now," she said quietly, hearing her voice crack.

Con uncharacteristically reached a hand out and tilted her chin up. "Not totally. You got me."

She nodded, then stood up from her chair and kissed him on the cheek, feeling his mustache brush against her face. Without warning, a rush of tears came, but she pushed them down inside and hugged him, inhaling the faint scent of limes from the soap he used to shave. He still used just a sharp knife and soap, and she never knew why he didn't use shaving cream. Or why he never got a microwave. Or why he ate his food cold, usually, as if he were still eating K rations.

"You got that brother of yours, too." Con pointed toward Danny. "He'd die before he let anyone hurt you."

"That, Con, is what I'm afraid of." She pulled away from him.

Maggie looked over at the urn and stepped toward it. She caressed it. Then she went to the ladder and climbed up into the loft. Con said he'd sleep in the chair by the fire. There was a thick mattress on the floor of the loft made up with flannel sheets and a down comforter. A small wood-burning stove stood in the corner. On one wall was a gun rack holding five different types of guns with long barrels, none of which looked like typical hunting shotguns, but rather like the types of guns snipers might use, Maggie thought. All had scopes. Against the other wall was a simple pine chest of drawers.

Maggie slipped off her shoes and walked to the chest. Three pictures were lined up in rectangular silver frames. The first was of herself, Danny and Con. They were sitting on a bench in Atlantic City. She had a box of saltwater taffy on her lap, and her legs dangled over the side of the bench, not quite touching the boardwalk. She was grinning, and Danny was in mid-laugh, his mouth agape and toothless. Even Con was smiling, one arm around each of them. The next photo was of a woman Maggie didn't know. She was Vietnamese, and she was very beautiful. The picture was so faded, it seemed almost sepia toned, but Maggie looked closely and realized the photo had been in color at one point. The final picture was of her father and Con. It looked as if it might have been taken during the Laos years, the Air America years, the years of a lot of cash and little information. They wore fatigues, but she could tell they weren't in the army. For one thing, her father was wearing a wedding ring, and her parents had been married after he'd been discharged. They didn't have on dog tags, either.

She took the picture from the dresser and moved to the mattress. The loft was dimly lit by the woodstove and a small lamp on the floor by the bed. Maggie unbuttoned her jeans and stepped out of them. She left her sweater on and lay down on the mattress, snuggling under the sheets and goose-down comforter.

Shifting herself with her elbows, she got closer to the lamp on the other side of the bed. She held the picture close under the light. She thought of Hop, Con, her father. They would have had to torture him, worse than what they'd done to Danny. She shut her eyes tightly, then opened them again. The picture was blurry now. In the quiet of the loft, she turned off the light and allowed the tears to come. And sometime near dawn, she finally fell asleep, dreaming of taffy and Atlantic City, but then its seascape changed to a rice paddy, and choppers began to chase her, the screams of her mother flooding her ears.

Chapter Seventeen

Danny woke near dawn. The cabin was quiet. He opened one eye, saw that Con was sleeping in the chair with a rifle across his lap, and Bobby on the floor, and then shut his eye again and pretended to be asleep. His head throbbed. He reached into his pocket for the bottle of painkillers he'd brought from Maggie's. He opened it silently, emptied three pills into his palm and swallowed them one at a time, using what little saliva he could muster. Then he settled back against the arm of the couch and tried to think as a vague numbness settled over him.

He remembered his mother. He and Maggie had shared a bedroom growing up, and his mother would come in and tell them stories about Vietnam. In her Vietnam, there was no war. In her Vietnam, there were beautiful rivers and tigers in the grass, gentle oxen and wise old grandmas who dispensed advice to the village. There was the day honoring your ancestors—the last day of January every year, and Maggie and Danny had very auspicious ancestors. In their mother's Vietnam, you could hear crickets playing their songs like violinists at night, tree frogs adding to the orchestra. She never mentioned bombs or napalm. She never mentioned a massacre. Or Tam.

He tried to imagine the pain she must have kept inside, and of course now a million things about her made perfect sense. Not the least of which was her suicide.

He and Maggie loved their mother so much. That she hadn't left a note, hadn't said goodbye, that she had doomed herself to hell in the Catholic world and to a terrible rebirth in the Buddhist one, plagued them.

Maggie had drank over it. Danny rarely spoke with his sister about Bobby, AA or quitting drinking. One day, she drank hard as the owner of the Twilight. The next, she didn't. She drank ginger ale.

He never talked to her about what had made her quit or why she'd felt she had to drink in the first place. He had never seen his sister drunk. Not the way people pictured alcoholics. Instead, she was quiet. She would sit up in her apartment alone and drink until she could fall asleep. He knew she couldn't sleep. Neither of them could. Not well.

Although these things went unspoken, he knew she drank to fill the void left, not only by their mother's death, but by the quiet torture of unanswerable questions. Every time he thought *why*, he would feel a stabbing pain in his chest. So Maggie drank, Danny ran.

He didn't run away. He could never leave his sister for long, or Hell's Kitchen. But he ran with his father, getting into trouble, going a thousand miles an hour, scheming. They'd hijacked a truck once, filled with electronics. They'd sold grenades once. They'd mostly fenced stolen goods, holding things until the heat had died down and then selling them, taking a cut of the profits.

Danny ran in perpetual motion. He'd done cocaine a few times until he'd realized he didn't need any help whatsoever with relentless alertness. Hypervigilance.

Now, lying on the couch, he thought of Calhoun raping his mother. Killing her village. The fucker would have to pay.

Danny had killed a man once. And that had been an accident. He and his father were scheduled to meet a guy who wanted them to hold onto some stolen jewelry for safekeeping. But the guy had snorted himself a sinus cavity full of cocaine and, Danny guessed, it was peppered with PCP or something because he suddenly pulled a tire iron out of the trunk of his car as they went to view the merchandise. His father reacted and reached for his gun, but the guy was so out of control, he used the tire iron like a bat and whacked Jimmy's arm, breaking it. Then he turned toward Danny and swung at his head. Danny ducked, took out his gun and shot him.

The gun wasn't traceable. The guy was a lowlife. Danny hadn't shed any tears over it. He'd killed a man. It had happened. Not because he'd wanted it to happen, but because that was the guy's karma. Sometimes, every once in a while, the dead man would come to him in a dream, but Danny pushed it way down and tried to forget. And he never wanted to kill again.

Until now. Because even if he had to go to prison for the rest of his life, there was no way in heaven or hell that he would let Calhoun go on breathing the same air as he and Maggie.

Danny clenched his jaw, then tried to relax into the painkillers. Eventually he dozed off again.

Sometime later, Maggie shook him gently.

"Danny?"

He stirred. "Yeah, bright eyes?"

"We've got to get down to Hop's."

Danny moved stiffly.

"Are you in pain?"

"Nah."

She didn't ask him why he wasn't. She was good that way—not like a lot of recovering alcoholics who preached. She'd seen him drunk; she'd seen him wasted on Percodan a time or two when he'd just felt like being a mess. Just felt like it.

"Bobby's called in for a week of sick time. Pulling some favors. I called up Tony T. He's going to open for me for a few days."

"He always steals from the till."

"Like I give a fuck right now. If he feels like taking a couple of hundred, let him."

"What if the bastards who messed me up show at the Twilight? Shouldn't we warn him?"

"Tony T.?" Maggie just smiled. "No. Maybe someone should warn the feds, but I'd rather think of them suffering."

Tony T. was a second cousin on their father's side. He'd served fifteen years in Dannemora. Danny remembered visiting day once, the prison rising like a fortress in upstate New York, half-shrouded in mist. Tony had killed a man—that was what he'd been caught for. But Danny knew the *T* stood for *Titanic*. Because beneath that conviction was a rap sheet and a dozen unsolved murders that somehow intersected with Tony, like an iceberg's hidden deadliness.

"Okay, bright eyes." He gingerly touched his cheek, and then felt along the stitches. "How ugly am I?"

She leaned over and kissed him on the forehead. "You'll never be ugly, Danny."

She held a hand out to help him up. He groaned for a second as he stood, feeling a tightness in his rib cage that made it hard for him to take a full breath. He still couldn't move the arm more than a few inches in any direction. His jaw hurt. His cheekbones. His eye sockets. There wasn't much that didn't hurt, even with all the drugs coursing through his body.

Con was percolating a pot of coffee over the small fire burning in the fireplace. Danny could never understand why someone who hated the war so much held onto habits from his time in country, but he'd never gotten a coffeemaker.

Danny walked over to the fireplace and, using his good arm, grabbed a mug from the mantel—right next to the urn filled with his father's ashes. He held out the mug to Con, who filled it with coffee.

Danny sipped the strong brew. "You still make the best damn cup of coffee."

"'Course I do. It's an art form." Con tugged on the end of his mustache.

Bobby emerged from the bathroom freshly showered and wearing what looked like borrowed clothing from Con, a Harley-Davidson T-shirt, with a flannel shirt over it.

"Have you called this Hop guy to tell him we're coming?" Bobby asked them.

Con shook his head. "You're better off just going down there."

"What if he's not home?"

Con snorted. "He'll be home. The Angel Tavern is open 365 days a year, including Christmas. He lives above it. Ain't never known him to take a day off."

Maggie went to wash up. She borrowed a sweatshirt of Con's. Then Danny went in the bathroom. It was the first time he'd looked at his face since the beating. The face staring back at him from the mirror wasn't his. Hell, if he didn't know his own face, he wouldn't have recognized himself. His eye was the worst. The eyelid was completely black, and it was still nearly swollen shut. Coupled with the stitches zigzagging through his eyebrow, he looked subhuman.

Danny gently washed his face. He took a few more painkillers and brushed his teeth with his finger, then rinsed three times with mouthwash. When he rinsed, he spat out blood clots from the gum where he lost his tooth.

He wished Maggie was out of this now. He hadn't known where to turn when he'd shown up at her place, but now, knowing the shit storm they were in, he hoped that the boyfriend cop at least loved her enough to make sure nothing happened to her.

Danny was perfectly willing to die in order to kill Calhoun. He knelt in the small bathroom and said a prayer.

Let me get him. But let her go free.

Chapter Eighteen

Vietnam, July 1972

Mai's mother died three days after the village massacre. The three of them—her mother, Mai and Tam—had remained hidden for hours after the Americans had left. When they'd finally emerged from their hiding spot, Mai had realized that the screams and gunfire, the sounds of death, were nothing compared to the smells.

Mai's mother had wandered, shuffling and dazed, passing a charred body here, a burning home there. The animals were all dead, burned alive. Mai feared she and her mother and baby would starve.

Jimmy. That was Mai's prevailing thought. She would get them to Saigon, where Jimmy had planned on taking them anyway. She would find him, or if not him, take Ma to *Tante's.*

But her mother wouldn't leave right away. They had all suffered a bad death. All of them. An entire village. A bad death meant a terrible rebirth. Her mother prayed to Buddha and spoke to the dead, urging them toward a good rebirth, toward light. Mai didn't think it would do much good.

Mai's mother would not sleep. Chanting, crying, talking, she rocked back and forth in a trance. She refused to rest. The second night after the massacre, Mai fell asleep on a makeshift bed of half-burned straw, Tam clutching her neck. When Mai woke up the next day, she did not hear chanting. She sat up and saw her mother was dead, her body already cool to the touch.

Mai stood over her mother's body. *Go to a good rebirth, Ma. Go…*

As she whispered prayers for her mother, Mai felt a desolation. She was left in a village of spirits and ghosts, a very bad energy all around. She was completely alone now, except for Tam.

Mai went to the hiding place and took her magic box, her other camera, and all the money Jimmy had given her. She had some blankets, a little charred, and she wrapped Tam in them and then tied her to her back. Magic box in hand, she started toward Saigon, not knowing if she could find Jimmy in the chaos of war.

Mai was afraid. She walked along worn paths and used the tall grasses to hide every time she heard a vehicle approaching. Blisters on her feet bled, and she was thirsty and more tired than she could ever remember being. She wondered why she didn't cry. She had left her mother to be eaten by wild animals. She had left her village. She had left the evil place. She felt dead inside.

The closer she got to Saigon, the more she felt the anxiety of hope mixed with terror. How could she find this one man in a city gone crazy? She would have to. *Tante* would help her.

Mai made her way to her aunt's apartment. She knocked on the door and her aunt's maid, an older woman with a severe gray bun, answered.

"*Bonjour*," the maid said. She wore a crisp black uniform with a white apron. Her skin was wrinkled and smelled of talcum powder.

Mai explained in Vietnamese what had happened. She glimpsed her aunt coming into the room, her silk dress swishing as she walked. She said something to her maid and dismissed the older woman with a wave of her hand. Mai marveled at how *Tante* had not aged at all. Not one crease on her face. If anything, she had grown more beautiful, all her girlish fat had gone, her face angular and exotic.

"Ma is dead," Mai whispered.

Her aunt's expression remained haughty and elegant, but her left eye twitched ever so slightly. "Come in," she said.

Mai followed her into the living room, but didn't sit down. She watched as her aunt looked over her ragged, soot-covered clothes, and glanced at Tam, her face angelic in sleep.

"I knew one day you would be my problem," she said coldly.

"I won't be a problem. I have to find Jimmy. He will fix everything."

Her aunt lit a clove cigarette, its spicy-sweet smoke filling the air. "A soldier."

Mai nodded.

Tante shook her head. "Is that his?"

Mai hesitated. "No."

"You can stay. The baby can't."

Mai clutched Tam to her chest. She could still smell the burned village on Tam's blanket, like the lingering scent of wood chips after a fire.

"No."

Her aunt tapped her foot. "My husband will not allow a child."

"Don't you even care how your sister died? What happened to our village? To your home?" Mai wanted to say more, but the words were stuck. The room was spinning.

Tante turned on her heel. She lifted a purse that had been lying on the dining-room table. She removed some money and left it on the gleaming dark wood table.

"Take it," she said over her shoulder. "And if you change your mind, you may return. There's an orphanage run by a French priest. You can leave her outside its gates."

Her aunt's heels clicked on the floor and she disappeared behind a hanging tapestry. Mai couldn't breathe. How was it possible that her own aunt was this way? Her mother had once called *Tante* a dragon lady. It was so.

Mai trembled. All she wanted was to wash, a place to sleep, clean clothes. She stared at the money on the table. Jimmy had given her plenty of money. And there had been money with the magic box, too.

Her aunt's maid entered the room again. She looked at the money then looked at Mai.

Mai started toward the door with Tam in her arms.

"Un moment," the maid whispered. Mai turned to face the

old woman who suddenly left the room. Mai waited, wondering what the woman wanted. When she returned a few minutes later, she handed Mai a shopping bag. Inside were clean clothes, a small blanket, candies, two bottles of soda and some fruit.

Mai's eyes watered with gratefulness. She took the bag and left the apartment. She changed her clothes hurriedly in the stairwell, her hands shaking. Mai wrapped Tam in the fresh blanket. But she refused to throw away their old things. She needed the smell of death on their clothes to keep her from thinking this was a dream.

She wiped at her face and ate two figs. Tam woke, and Mai fed her tiny pieces of fig. She opened a bottle of soda and got Tam to sip. Then Mai wrapped the rest of the fruit and their belongings into the large cloth that held the magic box. Making her way to the street, she looked left and right at the teeming sidewalks, listening to the cars, watching bicycles thread through the crowds. Then, carrying all she owned, baby on her back, she fell in with the people of Saigon. In the distance, she saw a temple. She would go there. Maybe once the smell of her dead village had dissipated in her mind and she had prayed, she would be able to find her soldier.

Chapter Nineteen

Bobby Gonzalez drove toward Asbury Park. Never in his life had he felt so utterly fucked.

He glanced over at Maggie, who was dozing. Then he looked in the rearview mirror at the back seat. Danny was passed out. Bobby knew he was swallowing painkillers like candy. Con had handed Danny an entire bottle of Oxy-Contin when they'd left.

Bobby hoped, without any real expectation, that the film would turn out to be a phantom. But Con hadn't struck him as someone who chased phantoms.

Maggie stirred. He reached over and squeezed her hand. "We're not too far away, baby."

She stretched, then stared out the window.

"You okay?" he asked.

"No."

He heard a catch in her voice.

She sighed. "When I think about what my mother went through...I feel so hopeless. She was the most beautiful

woman in the world. You know, she used to sing us lulla-
bies in Vietnamese. I wonder if she sang them to Tam at
one time."

"I can't believe you never knew."

"Now I can see it. The way she was always wanting the
gods to protect us. Jesus, Buddha, any god. But I used to think
it was the war that made her that way, never guessing it was
something so...awful. The war and something even worse."

"You realize the world of trouble we're in."

"You mean Calhoun?"

"Yeah."

Maggie looked out the window as she spoke, turning her
face away from him. "No. He doesn't realize the world of
trouble he's in."

A jolt of fear hit his stomach. "What do you mean?"

"I mean Danny and I will find Tam. And then we'll deal
with Calhoun. I'm sure he's behind my father's murder. And
he will pay. One way or another."

"That doesn't sound very Buddhist." He hoped to proj-
ect some calm over what was already a messed-up situation.

"No. It's not. But it's very Hell's Kitchen. It's very Jimmy
Malone."

Bobby shook his head. Jimmy Malone was in an urn. If
her father was a fraction as fierce as the rumors surrounding
him, that didn't bode well for their quest to find Tam and
the film.

"Tell me about Hop."

"Of the three of them, he's the craziest."

Thinking of Con's booby traps, the thought that Hop was
crazier wasn't comforting. "What do you mean?"

"I mean he's paranoid."

"And Con isn't?"

"Con is justifiably cautious. Hop is paranoid."

"You call C-4 and a man who talks about flesh hanging from the treetops justifiably cautious?"

"Yeah. In the world of my father. But Hop... He's nuts. Always has been."

"In what way?"

"Hating Asians. Hating half-breeds like me and Danny. He's missing a leg. Left it there, he says, and he wants everyone to pay until he gets it back."

"His leg?"

She nodded.

"He wants it back." Bobby let the sentence hang in the air, letting its very craziness fill the space between them.

"That's what he says."

"I don't feel good about just dropping in on this guy."

"He's okay. After my mother died, he was pretty protective of Danny and me. Even if we're half."

Bobby glanced over at her. "You know, I think you're the most beautiful woman in the world. Half. Whole. Does it matter?"

Maggie flipped down the passenger-side visor and looked at her reflection. "I look like my mother. I wonder if I look like Tam."

"You know you can't get your hopes up too much. If your father couldn't find her all these years—"

"Danny will find her."

"Why Danny?"

"Because that's what brothers do."

They took the exit for Asbury Park and headed toward the beach. They found a spot on the main drag and parallel parked. Maggie turned around and woke Danny.

"We're here."

He stretched and wiped some spittle that had gathered at the corner of his mouth. The three of them got out of Bobby's car.

"There it is." Maggie nodded toward the Angel Tavern. The light of late afternoon fell over the empty beach, and only a few bikes were lined up along the curb.

Bobby checked the place out as they approached. When they walked in, he immediately looked for the exits. The bar was nearly deserted except for some hard-core Hell's Angels sitting on a few bar stools, slumped over their beers. Two were playing a fractious game of darts.

The bar smelled of stale beer, and a few peanut shells crunched under Bobby's feet as he walked. Even in the day-time, it was very dark inside.

Danny waved at the bartender. Bobby sized him up. The guy may have been forty, but through hard living appeared sixty.

"Hey, Leroy. Is Hop around?" Maggie asked.

Leroy gave a nod of recognition. "Upstairs. Dogs are on the landing. I better call and tell 'im you're here."

Leroy picked up an old-fashioned rotary-dial phone and whispered something they couldn't hear over the Springsteen that was blaring through the speakers. After a minute, Leroy hung up and nodded. "You can go on up."

Bobby instinctively took Maggie's hand as they walked past bikers who were appreciatively checking her out. He never wanted not to be somewhere so much in his life.

They walked to the very back of the bar, then through an office, filled wall-to-wall with papers and cases of booze. They passed through another door and then ascended a narrow staircase with only a single lightbulb hanging at the top of the landing. Bobby heard dogs and prayed to God they were being put away somewhere. They didn't sound like Chihuahuas.

The door to the apartment opened, and there stood one of the biggest men Bobby had ever seen, his face in shadow, his large frame illuminated by the dim bulb.

"Dead or in jail?" the voice boomed down. "'Cause if you're here, it's one or the other."

"Dead," Danny said, his voice gravelly and dry.

"Who's the cop?"

Bobby blinked hard. Was it that obvious?

"Maggie's boyfriend," Danny said.

"He cool?"

Danny nodded.

They arrived at the landing. Up close, Hop appeared to be all muscle. Not steroid muscle, all ripped and anatomically perfect, but beer and hard-work muscle. Tattoos covered his arms like sleeves. Bobby recognized the dragon that Con had. It was fierce, its wings outstretched, every scale drawn in.

Hop grabbed Danny in a bear hug and clapped him on the back a few times. He stretched his arm out as a gesture of welcome. "You look horrible. Go on in."

He kissed Maggie's cheek. "I'm sorry."

She nodded and went in. Bobby stuck out his hand and introduced himself.

Hop initially ignored the hand. *Paranoid is right,* thought

Bobby. Then, in a voice so low that only Bobby could hear, Hop said, "You hurt her, I'll kill you." Only then did he take Bobby's hand.

As they entered the apartment, which was furnished in Salvation Army finds, Bobby could hear dogs snarling and barking like mad from behind a door.

"They're in their own bedroom, in the back. Can't come out without a key. They won't hurt you. Not without my orders anyway."

Hop lumbered down the hall. He said a command in what Bobby guessed was Vietnamese. The dogs instantly shut up. Clever, Bobby thought. No one who encountered the dogs—bad guys or cops—would know the commands except Hop.

The big man made his way into the living room where Bobby, Maggie and Danny sat down. Hop opened a battered metal filing cabinet. "Drink?"

"I'll take a Jack and Coke if you got it," Danny said.

Hop snorted. "I own a fucking bar, punk. Of course I got it." He looked at Bobby. "And you?"

"Coke if you got one."

"Me, too," Maggie said quietly.

Hop made them their drinks, pulling bottles out of the cabinet. Glasses, too. He got some ice cubes from the kitchen. He handed the drinks around. Then Hop poured himself a stiff scotch and sat down in a huge, worn recliner.

"Fuckers got him," he said with finality.

Danny nodded. "Not sure how, yet."

"You'll never find out how. They'll say he drowned in the Atlantic and he'll have freshwater in his lungs, or they'll say he committed suicide with no gunpowder residue on his hands. Won't matter. MEs can be taken care of by the agency."

"He's cremated already. We can't even exhume him," Maggie said.

Hop shook his head. He wore a long gray ponytail with a red bandanna around his head like a pirate. A few loose strands of hair fell across his face. "Wouldn't do you much good. You got to let go of it. He never believed your ma killed herself either, but he could never prove it."

The comment hung in the air, and Bobby looked over at Maggie and Danny. Both of them stiffened, as if the thought had not occurred to them before, but they let it pass.

"To Jimmy Malone." Hop raised his glass. They all saluted Jimmy and drank.

Maggie started, "Hop…we're here for the film."

"What film?"

She stared at him. Bobby could hear a clock ticking in the kitchen.

"You don't want it," Hop said softly.

"We do." Danny's voice was insistent.

"You don't. You don't know who these people are."

"We know it's Calhoun," Maggie said. "You can't protect us anymore."

Hop looked at them. "That film is a death sentence."

"She's our sister. Our mother." Maggie's voice was firm, and Bobby saw a different side of her. A woman he didn't know. Calm and full of grace. But most definitely as stone cold as one of her Buddha statues. Immovable.

Hop leaned forward, pulled a blue bandanna from his back

pocket and wiped at a bead of sweat that was dripping down his face.

"Dad must have told you that if he died the film belonged to us. That we'd come for it," Maggie argued.

Hop stood and paced. Bobby knew he'd lost a leg because Maggie had told him, but his walk did belie that fact. His stride was steady, even with a prosthetic leg.

Without saying a word, Hop went into the back bedroom, the one with the dogs. Bobby heard him giving assorted commands in Vietnamese. When he came out, about five minutes later, he held something wrapped in several scarves. He handed it to Maggie along with an envelope.

"The film. We made it into a VHS tape. The original is in a vault. The key is someplace else. The envelope has a bunch of pictures I thought you might want. The original film is my insurance policy. Dead man's switch."

"What's that?" Danny asked.

"It's an old term. It means that if some unfortunate accident happens to me, I've left instructions for getting that film to the *New York Times*. It means people like Calhoun have a vested interest in making sure I die of natural causes."

She nodded at him.

Suddenly, Hop sat down in the chair and wiped at his eyes for a second.

"I never hated you both for being half-breeds. Never. Not you."

"We know," Maggie said.

"Your uncle knows what happened to Tam."

Bobby watched as Maggie exchanged a look with her brother. Then she looked at Hop. "Our uncle?"

"In Boston. The college president. Your dad's brother. The fancy fucker."

"We know who he is, Hop," Maggie said. "But we've only seen him twice our whole life and our father hated him."

"You thought."

"What do you mean 'we thought'?" Danny asked.

"It's like the jungle, man," Hop said, smiling grimly. "You're bound to choke with all the weeds. All the deception."

Chapter Twenty

Saigon, September 1972

They sat in a Saigon bar as two listless go-go dancers twirled on the stage, their small Asian breasts different from the D-cup dancers at Jimmy's old haunt in Jersey.

"You have to find her, Con." Jimmy's face was haggard. He was already flying for the man with the dead eyes he now knew as Chief. Just Chief. And Jimmy knew Chief had vague military ties, and that he would disavow Jimmy if he were shot down.

"I'm looking. The village is gone, nothing but burnt grass, but the hiding spot is empty, and it looks like someone hid there. And her camera is gone."

"That means nothing," Jimmy said, downing his beer in two gulps. "They could have found her. Or someone else could have hidden there."

"No. She'd have been hiding there, Jimmy. You must have drilled it into her a thousand times."

"Then find her for me."

"I know you're nuts for this girl, Jimmy, but in case you haven't looked outside, man, there's a fucking war going on."

"And she's the only thing in this place keeps me sane. So help me find her, Con. I've got to fly tomorrow."

"I've got a contact." Con signaled for another drink. The beers were only mildly cold, condensation dripping down their green glasses.

"Yeah?" Jimmy raised an eyebrow.

"You ever hear of John Calhoun? He's assistant director of the agency. Word is the president sneezes and Calhoun's there holding the fucking tissue. His kid's here."

"Lemme guess. Sitting in a supply office somewhere getting his dick sucked while the rest of us wallow in blood and guts?"

"No. Seems the Calhouns trace their lineage back to the Civil War and past that to the *Mayflower*. Something like that. Long line of soldiers. The kid wanted to see battle. Now he's seen a little too much and the old man wants him in said supply office, only with a nicer title for the résumé."

"And what does this have to do with my girl, Con?"

"This guy's got contacts everywhere, and rumor is he's doing some of the old man's dirty business. Gimme a picture of Tam and Mai, and I'll see what I can do. It can't hurt."

Jimmy opened his wallet. It was a picture of Mai sitting on a blanket with Tam on her lap. The baby was grinning perfectly at the camera, even as Mai was staring off camera. Jimmy pulled the picture out of its clear plastic casing, feeling a pain in his stomach worse than what the two gooks had meted out to him in the hut. While he'd been lying in that hospital bed, Mai's village had disappeared.

"Here." He passed the photo to Con.

"I'll do what I can. Hop, too."

Jimmy sighed grimly. He rubbed his arm. "Chief wants me flying shit into Laos tomorrow."

Con shook his head. "Dangerous."

Jimmy nodded. He knew it was almost expected that he'd skim a little off the top. But when he'd realized he was flying heroin in his plane, making money to back the war with crap the people back home couldn't even imagine, he wanted to get in, get out, make his dough and get home—really home—back to New York, as soon as possible. It went without saying between him and Con and Hop that none of them gave a shit about communists.

A bar girl came over to the two of them. "You want go upstairs?" she asked Jimmy in broken English.

"No!" he snapped. He climbed off his bar stool and threw a five down on the bar. "Later, Con," he said to his friend, and pushed and maneuvered his way through the crowd of GIs, journalists and bar girls, until he got out onto the street.

His arm ached, but he ignored the pain and walked toward his apartment. He climbed the stairs and opened the door. Two rooms. Mai would have made it a home, but now it was nothing more than bare shelves, a table, a bed, a dresser. He stripped off his shirt and went to the bedroom and lay down on the mattress. The shutters on the window were only partially closed and a late afternoon sun filtered in. He turned on the fan by the bed. As it oscillated, he felt the breeze hit his face every few seconds, then the fan would turn and he'd feel oppressively hot again.

He held his arm up, his skin moist with sweat, letting the fan's breeze cool his sore arm for a moment. The dragon tattoo was there, rising like the phoenix.

He thought about his mother. She would have hated the tattoo. He smiled, imagining her slapping the top of his head, even as she would cook for him. She'd died when he was fourteen. She had suffered a heart attack climbing the stairs of their tenement. He had been at school when she'd died— in the bathroom, actually, sneaking a smoke with a buddy. Jimmy had suddenly thrown the cigarette in the toilet.

"What the fuck," his friend had said, turning around to see if a teacher had prompted the disposal of a perfectly good Marlboro.

"I don't know." Jimmy remembered shaking his head, fighting this nervous feeling. He couldn't explain it. Something was just *wrong*. When he'd gotten home two hours later, he'd been the one to find her body in the stairwell, her housecoat askew, groceries that had spilled out of the bag gathered at her side. The medical examiner had guessed her time of death to be around the time Jimmy had experienced his premonition.

Jimmy told himself that Mai was alive. If she had died in that hiding spot, he would have had another premonition, a feeling, something. She had to be alive. Had to be. Because if she wasn't, there was no reason to come home, except in a body bag.

Chapter Twenty-One

Maggie watched the film in Hop's living room, her fingers gripping the tweed couch cushions, her mouth dry, her chest tight. And as she watched it, she realized she was witnessing more than the destruction of her mother's village. She was watching her entire lineage, *her* relatives, being shot and burned, their children herded like sheep to slaughter. Her people.

Her whole life, as a Malone in Hell's Kitchen, it had been the Irish side that had dominated, save for the Buddhas in their apartment. St. Patrick's Day at the Twilight was a national holiday. She and Danny always got to skip school both on St. Patty's day and the day after when a hangover pallor meant no one would make sure they got up for school or ate their breakfast—at least after their mother had died.

When Maggie had looked in the mirror in her teens, she'd failed to see how exotic she was, failed to grasp how her face was hypnotic, how soon it would be something that changed a room. When she walked in, it was as if any party or any gathering quieted for just a split second. She'd seen her Vietnamese features, but she hadn't loved them, not yet.

As she'd grown past the awkward phase, she'd understood her features were different. As American culture had started to embrace black as beautiful and recognize, however feebly, ethnicity as a new form of beauty, she, too, embraced herself, the way her eyes turned up at the corners, the slight flattening of the nose, her long silky hair.

But now, watching the film, her mother's legacy was so much more than prettiness. It was more than the fat Buddha belly on the cash register. It was *this*. This massacre, the way her cousins and relatives—whose names Maggie would never know—had been killed, slaughtered, murdered. She felt herself, while sitting on Hop's couch, hold her head a little higher in her grief. They would be avenged.

When the film was over, Hop stood and brought the bottle of scotch over to the coffee table. No one said anything. Bobby stared at the television screen, even though Hop had turned it off. Danny's eyes were shut. Maggie felt as if a hive of bees had swarmed in her belly. For the first time in a long, long while, she wished she could take a drink. If she was honest about it, if Bobby hadn't been there, she would have. Fuck her damn sobriety.

The grief she'd felt when Con had told her that her father was dead was now crushing her. She felt as if she were being strangled.

"I'm sorry," Hop said, blotting his forehead with a bandanna again as he poured himself a drink. "Wish I didn't have this fucking thing. It's been nothing but a curse."

"Hop?" Maggie asked.

"Yeah?"

"Is there anything else we should know? Con says my father divided up the story. No one piece to any one man."

Hop's hands started to tremble. Maggie felt sick to her stomach. If someone like Hop was scared, things were going from bad to much, much worse.

"Well, shit." Hop took out his bandanna and blew his nose. "All's I can say is we didn't know. We thought Calhoun was…helping us."

"I know you never would have hurt her or my father, Hop. You were his best friend. You and Con."

"See, Con and me, we were in this—" He hesitated.

"What?" Danny asked.

"Whorehouse."

Maggie grinned despite herself.

"And then Con said we gotta meet this guy at the Continental Hotel bar. Some CIA director's son. About Mai. Now, I'll be honest, I didn't see what your father was so worked up over." Hop looked like he was at a loss for words, his face growing ruddy. "All right, so you know, they got my leg. I didn't like any of 'em. But Jimmy was hell-bent on bringing her back to the States. He hadn't even known her all that long. It was just fucked up all around, but I…" He held up the arm with the dragon tattoo. "Loyalty meant something. So we went to meet the fucker."

Maggie gritted her teeth. "Did he recognize her from the picture my father gave Con?"

"We helped him recognize her."

"What do you mean?" Danny asked. He leaned over and

grabbed the bottle of scotch and poured his glass near to the rim with it.

"Con showed him the picture. Said it was Jimmy's girl and her baby sister. He explained that they were in a village that got destroyed, and Jimmy had a hiding place for her and didn't think she was dead. Calhoun, cold as fucking shit, his face not registering a fucking thing, asked the coordinates of the village."

"And you gave them to him," Maggie said, horror filling her voice.

Hop nodded. "We did. I swear to you, we had no idea. We told him we were looking for her. That Jimmy had a bunch of money saved to get her out of there. And then—"

Maggie whispered, "Please, God, what?"

"And then we told him the reason we thought she survived—because the hiding spot was empty and her magic box was gone. And she was never without it."

A gasp flew from Maggie's mouth. Feeling overwhelmed, she stood and raced into Hop's bathroom. She dropped to her knees, feeling like she was going to vomit, and hung over the toilet bowl, quaking.

Eventually, the nausea passed so she got up and splashed water on her face at the sink. She looked at her reflection in the mirror. She wondered if Tam looked like her.

If they somehow found her, what would the grown-up Tam say? What if she was happy where she was and didn't want to learn about their mother?

"Baby?" Bobby rapped lightly on the bathroom door.

"I'm okay," she called out. Maggie composed herself and opened the door.

He immediately pulled her against him, his arms wrapped tightly around her, and kissed the top of her head. "We'll find her. We'll make sure he pays."

Maggie nodded, her head against his chest, then pulled back and returned to the living room. "I'm sorry," she whispered.

"No, I'm sorry," Hop said. "Shit, once we put it all together, years later, I went on the mother of all benders."

"I remember that bender," Danny said.

"So do I," Maggie added softly. Hop's bender had been legendary. He'd closed the Angel Tavern and had locked the doors. He'd given all his employees their final paychecks, plus something extra. He'd told them to come back in three months, if he was still alive, and if they still needed a job. Then Hop had proceeded to drink his entire stock—that was the legend, anyway. He'd sat, usually in the dark, jukebox on, usually Springsteen, and drank his way through the bar. He'd started with whiskey and bourbon, had moved on to vodka and scotch. Then he'd even drunk the weird stuff, like blackberry brandy, the shit people hardly ever asked for. Sometimes he'd drunk until he'd puked. And then he'd started again the next day. When he was done, he'd straightened out. Had the DTs pretty bad. Had even gone to a VA hospital for a week. Maggie remembered both Con and her father driving down, trying to help him to stop, getting him a bed in the hospital until he'd dried out a little.

"Hop, there's one thing I don't understand. Why my uncle?" Maggie asked. "We don't even exchange Christmas cards. Why him?"

"Two reasons. One…he's your father's brother. Jimmy always said that, even though they were different, they each had the other's back."

"And the other reason?" Bobby asked.

Hop didn't answer.

"What?" Maggie urged him.

"He was the one who picked up Mai when she came to America. She lived in his house until your father got home."

Chapter Twenty-Two

Boston, May 1975.

"Mai?"

Mai turned around and found herself face-to-face with a man who looked just like Jimmy. She smiled. "Hello, Terrence," she said, as clearly as possible in the English she had practiced repeatedly.

"Hello, Mai," he said, handing her a bouquet of roses as joyous airport reunions erupted around them.

Mai accepted the flowers and then looked around Logan Airport's terminal. "Where is Tam?"

"Tam?"

"My sister."

Mai saw the confusion register on Terrence's face, which was so much like Jimmy's, handsome with blue-green eyes. His hair was wavy, an auburn-brown. Mai knew Terrence was eight years older than Jimmy and that he was a professor of English. He didn't have the weary look of war on his face like his brother. Jimmy's eyes may have been the same color, but they were the perpetually tired eyes of a man who didn't sleep deeply or often.

"What?" she asked Terrence, an uneasy feeling building in her stomach.

She watched as he took a step toward her. He was wearing a gray suit, a crisp white shirt and a navy tie. He wrapped an arm around her. "Let's go over here, Mai, where we can talk."

Mai still didn't trust that all her paperwork meant she was really going to be allowed to stay, so she didn't make a scene. She was wearing her best dress, an American one Jimmy had bought her, in a simple black crepe with short sleeves, and she wore a black cardigan over her shoulders. She carried a purse, and the suitcase that she had checked contained all her possessions. The film from the magic box was in her purse. Jimmy still didn't know.

Mai allowed Terrence to lead her to the molded plastic chairs of one of the waiting areas, out of the concourse.

"Mai," he said softly, as she sat down. "There's been some sort of confusion. I got a phone call that Tam was not coming. That she was adopted."

Mai didn't know the word. She shook her head. "What that mean?"

Terrence sighed and took both her hands in his. "It means someone wanted to give her a home. To take care of her."

"Then we go get her."

"Something's wrong here. You didn't want her to be adopted by an American family?"

She shook her head furiously. "No, no. Where is she? We go get her."

"Okay, look, there's been some kind of bureaucratic mistake. We'll get this straightened out."

Mai again shook her head. "What that mean?" Her voice was more desperate now.

"We'll find her." He smiled at her gently, the same look she sometimes gave Tam when she wanted two pieces of candy instead of one. Terrence took her by the hand and led her through Logan Airport. They collected her suitcase and walked to the parking lot to Terrence's car.

Mai climbed in, marveling at the size and shininess of American cars, marveling at a thousand things from staircases that moved up and down, to buildings so tall they touched the clouds.

Terrence spoke as he drove. "I don't know how much English you understand."

"Some," she said.

"Okay. We'll find Tam. I'll make some calls tomorrow. I'll also try to get word to Jimmy somehow."

Mai stared out the window. She felt so lost. Nothing was familiar. Not the trees or the air. Nothing.

"I'll point out some of Boston's landmarks as I drive. Okay?"

He looked over at her and she nodded.

"Are you hungry?"

She was starving, but she was also trying not to collapse inside. She wanted to hold Tam. During the whole awful, crowded flight over, and throughout the mad, insane scene at the embassy, all of it, Mai had thought only of reuniting with Tam. It had sustained her like rice when she was hungry. She had imagined, over and over again, rocking her child to sleep in Terrence's house, which she pictured as an American castle. And now, none of this was coming true.

"A little," she whispered.

He reached over and took her hand and squeezed it. "Then we'll stop somewhere."

She nodded again.

Terrence drove through busy streets that were amazingly orderly compared to Vietnam. In her country, bicycles and motor scooters vied with cars and people and animals, and all of it noisy and disorganized. Here, red, green and yellow lights told the drivers what to do.

About fifteen minutes later, Terrence pulled into a parking spot on the street. He parked the car and got out, put coins in a machine, and then held open her door for her.

She shivered slightly.

"Jimmy said to get you some new clothes. Even in summer, the weather here is fickle. And wait until the dead of winter."

He wrapped an arm around her and guided her to a restaurant. When they stepped inside, a woman approached them and spoke to Terrence and then showed them to a table. The restaurant had polished hardwood floors, thick velvet curtains and crisp, white tablecloths. The napkins seemed as big as blankets.

Mai felt awkward. She didn't know what to say. Vietnam seemed so far away. She wanted Jimmy.

"My brother is crazy for you, you know," Terrence said and smiled, lifting his face over his menu. He had a dimple in his left cheek.

Mai blushed, then her eyes filled with tears.

"I know," he said soothingly. "Tam."

"Yes." The word choked off, and she pulled her napkin up to her face. She felt ashamed to cry in front of Terrence. He was a stranger, even if he was Jimmy's brother.

"I promise you… Look at me, Mai. Come on. Look at me."

She lifted her head slightly.

"I promise you, I will find Tam. This is…I don't know how to say it in Vietnamese. A mix-up. A mistake. A confusion. Um… We can fix it."

"Can you call Jimmy?"

"No, Mai. I can't. Not right now."

"He told me you had telephone. That I could talk to him."

Terrence smiled. "I do. But it's not that easy for us in the States to call Vietnam. We have to get an international operator. And Jimmy's not easy to reach. I've gone as long as five months without any word from him."

"Five months?" Mai felt her stomach clench.

"Oh, no, no… With you here, he'll call more. We'll talk to him. We'll get Tam."

A waiter came over and offered Terrence a wine list. He ordered a red and then asked for more time. Terrence interpreted much of the menu for Mai, and she chose a roasted-chicken dish. Terrence ordered prime rib.

Over dinner, he asked her a lot of questions about Jimmy and Vietnam.

"Jimmy says it rains a lot."

She shrugged. "Good for rice."

Terrence grinned. "Does my brother tell you what he does when he flies?"

"No. He flies things for a man named Chief. He gets

money. He saves money for us to have house someday. Here.
With Tam."

Terrence leaned back. "You must be a pretty remarkable
lady to tame Jimmy Malone."

"What that mean?" she asked.

"Jimmy," Terrence said with a wink, "was always the
wild one. Our brother, Michael, he died. He did a stretch
in prison. Was in and out of juvenile hall before that. He
was murdered when he got out of Sing Sing. Old score to
settle. But Michael, he was trouble in a bad way. I loved him.
But he was always so angry at the whole world. Jimmy, he
was wild in a way that he just made everyone want to be
around him. Had a way about him. Just a way. Fun. The
ladies loved him. And since he's met you, he's been a
goner."

Mai smiled, even though she didn't understand everything
Terrence said. Their dinners came, and Mai ate mostly in silence, letting Terrence talk about Jimmy's childhood, their
mother, Hell's Kitchen, a name she didn't understand. Why
would anyone want to live in a place named for something
so bad?

After dinner, Terrence drove them to his house. He had a
Dutch Colonial in Newton on an acre of land. He opened
the door and swept his arm to the side. "Welcome, Mai."

He switched on the light and Mai stepped into the front hall.
"How pretty."

Mai was astounded at how different Terrence's house was
from anything she was used to. *Tante* was wealthy, but this
house was more decadent. Thick Oriental rugs covered the
wood floors and dark wood furniture filled the living room

off to her left. A staircase ascended to the second floor, a crystal chandelier gleaming overhead.

"You must be exhausted," he said. He picked up her suitcase and started up the stairs. "The guest room is up here."

He made a right at the top of the landing and pointed to the bathroom. "That bathroom's all yours. I have one off of the master. And this—" he swung open a door "—this is your room."

He turned on the light. The guest room had a four-poster bed that was so tall, there was a stepstool to climb up into it. A thick goose-down comforter covered the bed, and a folded blue-and-white quilt rested at the foot of it in case she might get cold, he told her.

"Old Boston houses are pretty drafty."

He walked over to a mahogany vanity with a mirror. "This is for you. Make sure you unpack and treat this as your home."

"Thank you," Mai said. She walked over to the dresser and picked up a black-and-white picture in a silver frame. Three boys looked back at her from the photo. "This is Jimmy?" she asked. Pointing at the youngest one.

"Yeah," Terrence laughed. "I'm the knucklehead on the right."

She smiled at him.

"I'll leave you be for a while. You settle in."

He left and shut the door partway.

Mai looked around and fought back tears. She ached for Tam. She pulled her suitcase up onto the bed and opened it. Taking two stone Buddha statues, she placed them on the dresser. She put her clothes away and then pulled out pic-

tures of Tam and Jimmy, and the one photo her mother had
let her take of her.

Jimmy had given her a third Buddha, which was made of
jade. She put it on her nightstand. Then she knelt down on
the floor and cradled her head in her hands, praying to Buddha for help.

The door to the bedroom opened slightly.

Terrence didn't say anything. Mai was worried. Jimmy
had told her his family was Catholic. She watched Terrence's
eyes go from the Buddha, to her and then back to her again.

"Need anything?"

"No, thank you," she said, the *th* sound still virtually impossible for her to make, and came out more like a hard
t or *d*.

He stared at her, and she waited for him to speak.

"My brother is very lucky," he said. "You are very, very
beautiful."

With that, he shut the bedroom door. Mai didn't move,
or even breathe, until she heard his footsteps travel down the
hall. Then she cried for a long time, until no more tears
would come.

Chapter Twenty-Three

"Let's drive to Atlantic City for the night," Danny said. "We'll get a couple of rooms, and then we'll drive up to Boston tomorrow on some sleep and a meal. I gotta clear my head." He leaned back on the couch, feeling the unfamiliar sting of tears. "I got so much fucking shit crawling around in my brain, I feel like it's gonna bust out of my skull."

Maggie came over to him and brushed a lock of his hair off his forehead. He felt better at the touch of her cool hand on his brow.

"You guys better get off the grid," Hop warned. "Live like Con. No trace of nothin'. He don't collect no benefits, no bank account, no credit card, don't file taxes. Nothin' to put him on the grid. If you go to Atlantic City for the night, you better make sure you don't leave a trail."

"I'll use my credit card," Bobby offered. "Not them."

Danny raised his head and looked at Bobby. "Hop's right. And your card ain't enough, man. Not enough. These guys know you're with Maggie. They know everything about us. They want the film. They already killed the old man for it and left me in pieces. Come on, Bobby. Think like a criminal. Welcome to my world for a little while."

Maggie looked over at Hop. "How much cash can you spare?"

"I've got twenty thousand in my safe. You can have it all."

"We'll pay you back as soon as we're able to return to the Twilight. I have that much stashed in my bathroom wall."

Bobby looked over at Maggie with a puzzled expression, and Danny had to grin. He liked Bobby. He liked anyone who made his sister smile, which was a rare event. She had smiles for customers, and she knew how to work it for tips. Always had. But even Danny had to work for a real smile that traveled to her eyes. He would stockpile jokes and funny stories. Like the time he and the old man had thought they'd been hijacking a truck of flat screens, but it had turned out to be a truck full of Pottery Barn shit. As if he and the old man knew anything about decorating. Bobby made his sister smile. But he had no clue.

Danny didn't think that Bobby was dumb or anything. The detective had two citations, even. He'd shaken the hand of the mayor. Danny knew Bobby had elevated Maggie onto some kind of pedestal, but Bobby didn't know what lengths Maggie would go to to protect Danny and their father. Or how the law was optional to the Malones.

Maggie glanced at Danny. He gave a half nod of his head.

"Fine," she told Hop. "We'll take the twenty thousand."

Hop stood and went to the back bedroom again and returned with a lockbox of cash and a loaded Glock.

"Take it. You might need it. It can't be traced." Hop looked over at Bobby, who didn't say anything.

They got up to leave. "One more thing," Danny said.

"Yeah?"

"Do you think our mother killed herself?"

The question hung in the air for quite a long time. Finally, Hop spoke.

"When it happened, your dad didn't believe it. Then he found the film, and he *really* didn't believe it. He said she'd never fuck with her karma that way. All's I know is that I met your mother in country. She made me nervous."

"My mother made you nervous," Danny said, resisting the urge to laugh.

"Yeah. I thought she put some bad mojo or something on me, 'cause I'll tell you one thing, I ain't never met a woman more determined to find her man and take care of a baby than your mom. And the place got my leg."

"Coincidence, Hop. It's not like my mom took your leg."

"Yeah, well, she used to go pray for your dad. She'd talk to Buddha about him, and it was freaky. He never got so much as a scratch after that. Nothing. I mean, he'd fly into these hairy situations that no one could fucking get out of alive, but he would do his missions like he was just taking a stroll down the street, nice and easy. She started getting superstitious. She would say the same prayer every time. Your dad, he made it out in one piece. Me? My planes were always falling apart. They got my fucking leg. Anyway, do I think she killed herself? No. 'Cause she had some powerful magic."

Danny looked at Hop, who was deadly serious. He wanted

to argue with him. This wasn't a very logical reason to think she hadn't committed suicide. But then again, nothing about any of this was logical.

Maggie kissed Hop goodbye. Hop clapped Danny on the back and shook Bobby's hand. The three of them, like some weird Mod Squad, descended the staircase into the Angel Tavern and got into the car. Danny felt around in his pocket for the Buddha he carried with him. He stroked it and prayed his mother's mojo would keep them all safe.

Chapter Twenty-Four

Bobby Gonzalez drove to Atlantic City constantly checking his mirrors for anyone following them. Danny leaned in from the back seat, offering commentary as they approached the beachfront area.

"This place used to be so seedy when we used to come out here. But we thought it was the coolest place on earth. The diving bell. The wax museum. Remember that, Maggie?"

"I remember the diving bell, but I don't remember the wax museum."

Danny tapped Bobby on the shoulder. "Hey, I think we'd better stay at a small motel. All the big ones have a lot of security cameras and security people. They're paid to notice things."

They decided to stay at a place called the Seagull Motel and paid cash for two rooms. Bobby told Danny to keep his face down. A guy with that many stitches would be pretty memorable.

Their rooms were side by side and decorated in tacky

beach chic. Maggie and Bobby's room even had fishing net tacked to the walls for decoration.

Danny poked his head in their room. "Charming. Love what you've done with the place. I'm going to crash."

Bobby smiled at Danny's attempt at humor. "Before you go, give me a list of stuff you want. I'll go to a Wal-Mart or something. We need clothes, toiletries."

Danny wrote down his sizes and a short list of essentials, then went to his room. Bobby took a list from Maggie. Then he drove to a Wal-Mart and bought shampoo, toothpaste, toothbrushes, a blow-dryer, hairbrushes, and a few shirts, jeans and socks for him and Danny, and a couple of jogging suits, socks and sneakers for Maggie. As he stood holding up a soft black-velour tracksuit, he smiled to himself. He liked shopping for her. It was so normal, and the past couple of insane days had been anything but. He loved her body, the way her breasts fit perfectly in the cup of his hands.

He shut his eyes for a minute and just wished he could wake up in her apartment, lying in bed with her. They would work on the Sunday *Times* crossword puzzle together. He wondered if they would ever be able to do that again. Somehow, seeing Hop and Con and the rightful paranoia the film wrought in them, he started to have visions of a life always looking over their shoulders. It was as if their existence had been set in the middle of a field filled with landmines. They would never be able to take a truly confident step again.

As he paid for the purchases and drove back to the motel, Bobby tried to think clearly. Senator Calhoun was a third-term Republican from Indiana. He had burst onto the national scene maybe a decade before with whispers of a vice presidential nod. Now he seemed poised for the top job it-self. However, he had trotted out his Vietnam service as an issue against his main rival, who had served Guard duty dur-ing Vietnam, and the race was growing uglier by the day.

Calhoun had received a Purple Heart for the burns he'd sustained on his body and neck during an intense battle over a scrubby hill. Unlike a lot of vets who were somewhat re-luctant to discuss their service, Calhoun had a PR-perfect pitch down pat. Add a picture-perfect younger wife, whom he'd met at a Republican fundraiser, and you had the future First Couple. Calhoun's wife, Patricia, had a pedigree as im-pressive as Calhoun's. Her father was a mover and a shaker in the party. They had two children. The son was carrying on the Calhoun tradition by attending Virginia Military. The daughter was a high-school student with her sights set on Yale, dear old dad's alma mater.

Bobby was willing to cut men who had fought in war some slack. He'd once shot a kid. Mike Jimenez, age seven-teen, had just exited a bodega after holding it up. Bobby and his partner at the time were cruising the block when they saw him running. Bobby knew something was up, and the bodega owner came running out at the sight of their car, cursing and crying, claiming the kid had pistol-whipped him. Bobby took off after the kid on foot, yelling, "Freeze, police!" at the top of his lungs. Then—and Bobby had re-played the scene a thousand times in his mind—the kid, in-explicably, stopped in his tracks, turned around and pointed his gun at Bobby. What followed was a ten-minute standoff, with a crowd gathering, heckling as only New Yorkers can. And just when Bobby thought he'd talked the kid into dropping the gun, Jimenez fired into the crowd, grazing a woman, and Bobby shot him.

The inquiry was brief. Bobby was off desk duty in less than a month. But he drank over it. He'd seen the bottom of a fifth of Wild Turkey more often than he cared to recount. The kid's face had haunted him. He had worn an expression both scared and reckless as he'd pointed his gun.

So Bobby was willing to forgive much of the chaos of war. The split-second decisions men make in the heat of battle, screams of the dying in their ears, gunfire—real gunfire that makes your heart pound so loudly you think your rib cage might explode. But what he saw on the film was inexcusable. That was a bunch of guys gone wild with bloodlust.

Bobby had a couple of friends at the FBI, but he didn't dare call anyone. He knew he was in over his head, but he didn't know where to turn just yet. He thought of contacting the *New York Times*. But until they found Tam, he wondered if that was the best idea. If Calhoun knew where Tam was—and they had no idea if he did or not—he might just have her killed, too, without leaving a trace, and then all they would have was a lot of conjecture and a film that was very damaging, but also grainy and confusing. Maggie's mother was dead. They had nothing. How could they find one baby, now grown, all these years later? And how would she react when she discovered she was a child of rape?

He arrived back at the motel and walked to his and Maggie's room. He entered with his card key, and she was watching television, knees bent against her chest, covers tucked up near her neck.

"Hey baby." He put the plastic bags of purchases on the dresser. "Here's everything you asked for. I even bought you a sexy garter belt."

"You did what?" she laughed. "In the midst of all this, you want me to dress up?"

"I'm just kidding." He slid off his jacket, unbuttoned his jeans and took off his shirt. He wriggled out of his pants, leaving on his boxers. Then he slid into bed with her and pulled her against him, kissing her. He leaned his head back and she nestled into the hollow of his neck.

"You know we're in a world of shit, right?" he whispered.

"Mmmhmm."

"You know I love you. I'd follow you to the ends of the earth. I'd follow you to Vietnam if that's where this takes us."

"I know. I love you, too."

"Tell me about your uncle."

She sighed. "Terrence Malone, president of Manchester University. Tastes run to antiques and collecting rare editions of Milton, which was his area of expertise before he started running the damn place. First PhD is in English. Second is in comparative religion."

"Real dumb guy, huh."

"Yeah. I don't really know Uncle Terry at all. My father never talked about him. I vaguely remember him at my mother's funeral. An occasional phone call."

"Married?"

"Nope."

"So we're just going to show up."

"It worked for Hop."

"What do you think your uncle knows?"

Maggie shrugged. Then she sat forward and removed her shirt. "Can we make love, Bobby?"

She leaned in toward him and kissed his lips, and in an instant, he was hard. Their lovemaking felt, to him, urgent and intense, like the night they'd met at AA.

Afterward, she fell asleep first. They had left the television on, volume almost on mute, and he watched her in the flickering bluish light until his own eyes grew too heavy to keep open.

When morning came, they heard a frantic pounding on their door.

"It's Danny!" came the shout from the other side.

Maggie sat up hurriedly and put on her shirt. Bobby pulled on his boxers and stumbled toward the door, opening it as fast as he could.

Danny came barging through the doorway, grabbing the remote from the foot of the bed and clicking over to a different station. Then he turned the volume up, the bar of sound increasing across the screen.

Danny suddenly rocked back on his heels. "Jesus Christ," he cried. "Jesus fucking H. Christ."

Bobby and Maggie looked at the television. A camera taking film from a helicopter was panning back. Then the news program cut to the studio where a female newscaster looked straight into the camera.

"We're still waiting to hear more about that five-alarm blaze in Asbury Park. It appears the landmark bar, the Angel Tavern, has burned to the ground, and there has been smoke and fire damage to two surrounding buildings. The cause is labeled as suspicious, and we'll bring you updates as we get them."

Bobby walked over and shut the door, which was still ajar. Then he went to the nightstand and locked and loaded the Glock and handed it to Danny.

"Shoot to kill. Ask questions later."

He looked over at Maggie and wondered how it was possible to love her so much and to feel so utterly and completely abandoned by the rest of the world.

Chapter Twenty-Five

July 1975

Mai awoke in the middle of the night. She had been in America two months now and still she could not sleep well. Her stomach was constantly upset from eating American food, and the quiet of Terrence's house was eerie.

Even before the war, Vietnam had been alive with sounds. Americans lived choked off from nature, Mai decided, from the sounds of the night, even the wind and rain. When she and Tam had lived with Jimmy in Saigon, the city had been full of noise. Lots of it. And in the temple, there was chanting. But Terrence's house seemed dead, and she took that as an omen.

Sighing, she rose and opened her bedroom door a crack. Peering down the hall, she could see a light coming from downstairs. She crept down the hallway in her bare feet, wearing the flowered flannel nightgown Terrence had taken her shopping for, then she slowly descended the staircase. At the landing, she saw Terrence working at a typewriter in his office.

"Mai," he said as he looked up and smiled at her, "come in." He moved a small pile of books from the chair beside his desk and gestured for her to sit down. "Can't sleep again?"

She nodded as she sat down, tucking her legs beneath her and crossing her arms over her chest. "Why you never sleep either?"

"I'm working on my book."

She looked at him, waiting, as she usually did, for him to explain himself. Jimmy knew some rudimentary Vietnamese, and she had taught him more, and he had taught her what little English she now spoke and understood. But Terrence knew no Vietnamese at all, so he often worked to fill in the blanks by talking more, and sometimes, comically she thought, louder. Eventually, he'd say enough that she'd recognize a word or string of words that would allow her to understand.

"Milton." He opened a book and showed her a picture. "He lived a long, long time ago, and he wrote about hell. Do Buddhists have hell?"

She shook her head. "No. But I know what it is. Bad place."

"Right. So he wrote a book about a journey to hell, and people like me teach about it."

"He go there?" She was puzzled.

"Who?"

She pointed at the man in the pen-and-ink drawing. "Mil—ton," she said hesitantly. "He went there? Hell."

Terrence smiled at her. "No. He imagined it and wrote

about it. A terrible place." He reached out and took her hand. "Is there anything I can do to make you happy? You know…happy?" He exaggerated a smile.

She shook her head.

"You got another letter from Jimmy today. Do you want me to read it to you?"

"Yes."

"Go get it then," he said softly.

Mai jumped up from the chair and raced upstairs to her nightstand, opening the drawer. A dozen letters lay, all in the thin onion skin of airmail envelopes, with the colorful stamps of Vietnam. Each was as perfectly neat as the day it had arrived from the post. She took the new one and brought it down. Jimmy had mailed letters before she'd even left, so they would be waiting for her. She could read little English, though she practiced writing her name. Thankfully, Terrence read them aloud, his voice soothing, sounding so much like Jimmy's. If she shut her eyes, she could almost imagine him there with her.

She walked back downstairs and thrust the letter toward Terrence, her hand trembling a little.

"Someday," he said, his face looking sad, Mai thought, "a woman is going to love me so much that her hands shake to get my letter."

She didn't understand, but she sat next to him again and waited.

Terrence opened the envelope with great care, pulling out the thin, unlined paper. He unfolded the letter very carefully. "I know you keep them like museum objects," he whispered.

When she looked confused, he said, "Never mind." Then he began to read.

Dear Mai,

I love you. This place has gone stark-raving mad. I live my life in two extremes. Either flying under the worst conditions, or missing you. That's all I know. Those two things. And now, I'm looking for leads on Tam.

Please don't be afraid. We'll find her. And Terry will take good care of you.

Think good thoughts. Like the time I brought you bubble gum and taught you how to blow bubbles. Or the time you tried to teach me how to catch that crazy chicken of yours.

I wish I could write fancy like my smarty-pants brother. But I can only write like me, Mai. You know I had a tough life as a kid. And I can't say it's a picnic doing what I do over here either. I've seen stuff I could live to be a hundred and will never be able to forget. Neither will you, of course.

But think of it, Mai. Two people on opposite ends of the earth, with no reason to ever come together, and in the midst of that insane war, we did. It was fate. We're going to have a long and healthy life together, Mai. You're my girl.

Love,

Jimmy

Terrence neatly refolded the letter and handed it back to Mai. She rubbed it against her cheek. She understood words like *bubble gum* and that the war was sad. But more importantly, she understood the part where he said she was his girl.

"Thank you, Terrence," she said.

"Now you'll be able to sleep, right? Put it under your pillow."

She stood and said, "I go up now." She leaned down and kissed his cheek. When she walked away, she again thought that he looked very sad. Terrence's eyes were starting to be as forlorn and tired as Jimmy's. It was as if she could look into Terrence's eyes and see his brother reflected back.

Chapter Twenty-Six

Vietnam, July 1975

Father Damian Bouchet liked a nice port. If it wasn't available, he'd drink nearly anything else—except for rye, which for some reason, he'd once told Jimmy, his liver couldn't seem to handle. Jimmy arrived at the orphanage, which was in chaos as rumors flew of the North Vietnamese killing people in the streets. But Jimmy came at midnight and found Father Damian sitting in his office, poring over papers.

"Port," Jimmy said, holding a bottle aloft, standing in the open doorway. "Care to have some, Padre?"

Father Damian looked up, startled. "What are you doing here? Are you crazy?"

"Well, I'm a little crazy. So how 'bout it? Port?"

Father Damian licked his lips. "Sure, Jimmy my boy, sure."

Jimmy walked over to the chair opposite Father Damian's desk. He reached behind the planter on the window ledge and found two semi-clean jelly-jar glasses that were hidden there. One looked as if it had held booze of some kind at one point and hadn't been washed since. But Jimmy figured the port would disinfect the glasses. No harm, no foul.

He pulled out his Swiss Army knife and used the corkscrew to open the bottle. Then he poured Father Damian a tall glass. He handed it across the desk and then poured himself one. Then Jimmy watched the priest as he took his first sip.

Father Damian had the perpetual shakes of a man always a port or two away from the DTs. His hair had long since turned white in his years tending to the orphans of Vietnam. His face was fairly unlined for a man of seventy, though his nose was always the red and mottled purple color of a true alcoholic.

Jimmy knew the sisters ran the place. Sister Bernadette was the gentle one. Jimmy swore she was like the Ingrid Bergman character in *The Bells of St. Mary's*. Jimmy's mother had been a sucker for Bing Crosby movies. She had luminous skin and pale blue eyes that he swore sometimes turned violet when she was sad. Sister Catherine had the thin, pinched look of a more stereotypical nun. She was stricter, though Jimmy knew she had a soft spot for the orphans with cleft palates. They were doomed to grow up in isolation behind the walls here, or worse, now that the North Vietnamese were taking over.

"Somehow, I don't think this is a social call," Father Damian said.

"You've been here too long, Padre. You know all the angles."

Father Damian tossed back the rest of his drink in one

shot and then held out his glass for more. Jimmy filled it, but then, without warning, reached across the desk and grabbed the old man by the wrist that held the glass, squeezing it mercilessly.

"Who bought you?"

"What?"

"Tam. I told you that baby had to get out of here. I gave you more fucking money than this place will ever see in a year for her to have papers. What the fuck happened?"

"I have no idea what you're talking about," the priest said hoarsely. "Let me go."

"I can sit here all fucking night, old man." Jimmy increased the pressure around Father Damian's wrist.

"Your language...your language, Jimmy."

"Look me in the eyes."

The priest did, and Jimmy saw the fear there. But he also saw resignation. The priest had been in Vietnam long before the U.S. had put its first marines on its muddy soil.

"Jimmy," the priest pleaded, "please. What's gotten into you?"

"I'll snap your wrist like a twig. Tell me who bought you."

Jimmy weighed in his mind whether he could actually go through with snapping the priest's wrist and decided he could. Catholic or not, burning in hell or not, he could. He realized he owed God something for saving him, but the priest was corrupt and a drunk, so maybe that would mitigate things when he finally met his maker.

"All right," the priest said, as his eyes involuntarily teared from the pain.

Jimmy released Father Damian's wrist and sat back down

in his chair. "Tell me. And just know that I'll come back and slit your throat while you sleep if I find out you've lied."

"You'd kill a priest? Is that what the war has turned you into? A murderer?"

Jimmy smiled coldly. "Save me your sanctimonious crap. You're a smuggler and a profiteer."

"I rescue children."

"Yeah, well, rescue your own soul. What happened to Tam, and who bought you off?"

"Tam is dead."

Jimmy pulled a gun from his waistband without warning and aimed it right at the old man's head. "You're lying."

"Blowing my brains out all over my desk will only leave a mess for the good sisters to clean up, and you'll waste a fine bottle of port, for they'll surely pour it down the sink. But it won't change things."

"You're a fucking liar. A fucking liar!" Jimmy fought to keep calm.

"I'm not lying. She was to be picked up by a representative from an adoption agency, a man who was bought off by some of the funds you so generously gave as a donation to the orphanage. He says she was dehydrated from the flight. She'd gotten dysentery. He took her to a hospital and she died."

"What hospital?"

"Jimmy, going to the hospital won't get her back. And it won't do much good since she was flying under a false name."

"No. She's not dead. I can't tell Mai that. Not after all we did to get her to the States." Jimmy lowered his gun, then thought better of it. "No. You were bought off."

"Why? By whom? What makes you think that?"

"My brother says he was tailed by two men who looked like spooks. Back in Boston."

"Perhaps someone doesn't like your brother's politics. Perhaps he's made an enemy or two."

"My brother doesn't *have* politics. He has books and he has school."

Father Damian shrugged and smiled calmly. "You have no politics either, but that doesn't mean a great many people don't want to know what you're up to."

"No. Tam can't be dead."

"Jimmy," the priest said hoarsely. "Why would... Spooks? The agency? Who? Why would they want Tam dead or disappeared? Answer me. She's no threat to your government's plans. No threat to what you're doing in Laos—yes, I know. Like the eyes of God that see everywhere, I see a great deal, and hear a great deal."

"I think they want me to keep doing what I'm doing, no questions asked. And keeping Tam until I'm done guarantees that."

"Jimmy, put down the gun. I swear on my own life, no one came here to inquire about Tam. No one knew."

Jimmy shook his head and tucked his gun back into his waistband. "I don't know what to think anymore." He swallowed his port and poured another.

"This country, Jimmy, has seen more death spilled into her rivers than nearly any country on earth. It's filled with mosquitoes and heat and a rainy season that drives men insane. Disease. Tam died because of that, not because of spooks and the agency. It was God's will."

"Just the same, could you write down the name of the hospital for me. Just the same…"

Father Damian nodded and wrote the hospital's name on a slip of paper. Then the two men sat and finished the entire bottle of port. Jimmy ended up sleeping in a chair. When he woke the next day, hungover and with a dry mouth, the priest was gone, likely visiting all the children he truly did love. And Jimmy was left with something even worse than a hangover. A nagging feeling that something wasn't quite right.

Chapter Twenty-Seven

Maggie stared out the window of the car as Bobby drove toward Boston. They listened to the radio, an all-news AM station, and there was no word yet on whether Hop had died in the blaze. She had tried calling the cell phone Con sometimes used, but he hadn't answered. She felt herself sinking, just like in the diving bell.

The film was on her lap. Now that they had seen it, they were as good as dead. She struggled to think like her father.

When he had come back after the war, after his years in Laos, he hadn't hidden. Con had told her once, a few years before, that Jimmy had defied someone named Chief. But for whatever reason, Jimmy had lived out in the open, as if to say he wasn't scared of anyone, and he'd been left alone.

What would her father do in her position? Would she find Senator Calhoun and confront him? Hop had said he'd done a dead man's switch. She knew the term. If Hop turned up dead, the film would be found or sent to someone who could expose the whole thing. As long as Hop was alive, they

88888

were in a balance of power. So what did it mean that his place was burned to the ground?

She looked over at Bobby. He hadn't signed on for this. All her life, she'd kept men at arm's length. It wasn't like she wasn't hit on every night of her life. She worked in a bar, for God's sake. But a lifetime with and without her father had kept her wary. He had so many secrets. Of course, now it all made sense. In that apartment, with them always, was Tam. Her presence. She was there in the way their mother had always looked under the bed before saying good-night. Maggie had wondered sometimes if their mother had been insane. She'd committed suicide and had left no note. She'd been so superstitious that Maggie and Danny had lost track of all the things they were supposed to do, which shoulder to throw salt over.

Her mother's beliefs were so cobbled together. It wasn't as if throwing salt was something she'd learned as a child in Vietnam. Mai Malone had simply adopted *all* superstitions. So when she'd looked under the bed, when she'd crossed herself three times while speaking of the dead, when she'd leaped into the East River, Maggie had made whatever fragile peace she could with it by believing her mother had been insane. This jigsaw religion of two halves—East and West—fears of bogeymen and ghosts tossed in for good measure, was insane. In her mother's world, Satan existed. He could be anywhere—in a priest's soul or a homeless man's crazed eyes. Cats were lucky. Jesus and Buddha were brothers.

Her father's world was always anything but insane. It was cold and decisive. She knew he had it in him to kill people. She knew whatever he believed in, whatever spirits, if you were a bad man and you crossed Jimmy's path, you had to expect earthly payback.

Maggie bit her lip and looked out the car window again. It pained her to think that she had doubted her mother like that. She longed to talk with her, to ask her questions, to solve this mystery that had now taken their father and possibly Hop. But, like a séance, she would have to speak to her through mediums. Through Con, Hop, her uncle Terry, through people who could speak for Mai. And somehow she and Danny and Bobby would have to divine what to do next.

She looked over her seat at Danny.

"Out cold," Bobby said.

"He still can't move that arm much."

"I know. He needs a doctor. We don't know if he's bleeding internally."

"He's taking the antibiotics from Con."

"And a lot of painkillers."

"What's that supposed to mean?" she snapped.

"Nothing. He's just in and out all day long."

She wiped at her eyes. "I'm just worried."

"I know. Listen, did your dad ever use a doctor who...specialized in gunshots? You know, someone who wouldn't report the wound, took cash, that kind of thing?"

She tried to think. "Not that I recall. I mean, I'm sure he knew people who did that, but I wouldn't know how to find them."

He reached his right hand over and squeezed her hand. "We'll get through this."

"I wish I could ask my mom some questions. I wish I could ask my father. I feel like I'm walking through a minefield."

Curling up against the car door, Maggie drifted off to sleep. A couple of hours later, Bobby shook her awake. "We're near Boston. Now what?"

"What time is it?"

"Almost four."

Maggie turned around and roused Danny. He leaned forward. "Got a soda or something?"

Maggie reached down and dug a bottled water out of her purse. She'd bought it and some snacks at a gas station's minimart. She passed the water back to Danny, who opened it and drank quickly. Maggie watched as he took out his painkillers and popped two. She said nothing.

Bobby spoke softly, "Danny, how are you really feeling? Do you think we need to take you to a doctor?"

"And what? Explain the homemade stitches running through my face? I don't think so."

"Just watch the pain pills."

Maggie looked at her brother. He hated being told what to do.

"Don't worry about my fucking pain. Just worry about getting us to my uncle's."

Not wanting a fight, Maggie reached back and rubbed Danny's good arm. He was so much like their father, always just a touch on edge, always looking for an enemy in the grass. "How should we track down Uncle Terry?"

"Can Bobby call someone to get an address? A cop or something?"

Maggie looked over at Bobby. Taking out his cell phone, he dialed a number. Maggie listened as he told whoever it was that he needed a favor.

"I don't want anyone flagging this. I just need you to get me a home address for Terrence Malone in the Boston area. President of Manchester University. I think he might live in Newton. I'll call you back in ten."

Bobby pulled into a gas station. Maggie got out to use the restroom. When she came back, Danny was stretching his legs. Bobby was sitting in the car, talking on his cell phone.

Danny motioned her to him.

"Yeah?"

"Look, I don't know what the old man did in Laos. I don't know what kind of shit he was flying in. But I do know those guys and Calhoun, the people who want that film, and the people who wanted Dad dead, are fucking serious. So we have got to make sure we've got our backs covered 24/7. I'm only going to ask you this once, Maggie. Can we trust Bobby? I mean totally?"

"He gave you a loaded Glock and said shoot to kill. What do you think?" she snapped.

He nodded. "I thought so."

She reached out a hand and very gently touched the brow of his injured eye. It felt hard and melon-like, still swollen. "I'm worried."

"You and me both."

"I wish Con was here."

"If Con was here, there'd be dead bodies from Atlantic City to Boston, to fucking Laos for all we know. But yeah, I wish Con was here."

"If we find Tam, do you think she'd want to know us?" The question stuck in Maggie's throat. A sister. Their whole life, she and Danny had been like twins. A duo so tight no one had dared come between them on the playground, in school, and even later when they'd each begun to date. She was both scared of being a triumvirate and scared of being rejected.

He shrugged. "We'll always have each other, Maggie. You and me. But even if she doesn't want to have anything to do with us, she deserves to know her mother loved her and maybe even died for her. She deserves that."

Maggie reached out and squeezed his hand. The two of them went back to the car and climbed in.

"I've got an address," Bobby said, "and some directions my buddy read off to me from MapQuest. So here goes."

Bobby drove through the increasingly congested rush-hour traffic. It took them an hour and fifteen minutes to get to the house.

Danny let out a whistle. "Jesus, I guess being president of a university pays well."

They were at the gates of a mansion that sat atop a rolling hill. The house was made of fieldstone and chimneys jutted out of the slate roof on each side. Tall oaks dotted the front lawn, and in the back of the house, they could see woods. A gravel driveway snaked up to the front doorway. A wrought-iron gate and a stone wall fronted the street. Bobby hopped out and pushed it open.

"It was unlocked," he said as he climbed back in the car.

They drove up toward the house. Maggie cringed at the noise they were making. It wasn't as if she expected to sneak up on her uncle, but the tires crunched on the stones.

Bobby parked the car a few feet from the tall, wooden

double front doors, which had a stained-glass window in Frank Lloyd Wright's style above them.

The three of them climbed out. Maggie noticed her brother and Bobby both patting their guns and looking around. They walked to the front door and rang the bell, a heavy chime. They waited.

"I guess he's not home," Maggie whispered. "Should we wait for him to come back? Or we could go to a hotel."

Maggie pondered what would be their best option. And then, suddenly, they heard a dead bolt being opened. The door swung wide, and there stood their uncle, looking very much like their father.

His eyes traveled from Maggie to Danny, and then he whispered, "I knew someday you'd come."

Chapter Twenty-Eight

Thailand, December 1975

Jimmy Malone was going home. With any luck, he'd be kissing Mai underneath the mistletoe.

America had lost. Saigon had fallen, and even the secret war in Laos had failed. General Vang Pao had fled to Thailand, and the Khmer Rouge had taken over the merchant freighter *Mayaguez*. President Gerald Ford had sent in the marines. In short, America was fucked.

Sitting in a bar in Thailand, Jimmy wondered just how much he was going to have to look over his shoulder once he got back. Old scores people had to settle. People he had pissed off.

One time, before Saigon fell, Jimmy had been flying another nighttime rice drop over Laos. Con, his usual copilot, was grounded with the most hellacious stomach flu, and had told Jimmy he thought death by torture would be more favorable.

His copilot that night was a guy Jimmy didn't know well,

who went by the nickname Razor. Jimmy didn't trust him. He didn't trust anyone, except Con and Hop.

"There," Razor said, nodding at their drop point. It was dark as shit, but they knew there was a mountain trail below them.

Jimmy released the bales of rice and banked to his left. Twice in the past he'd known he was likely dropping opium for the heroin trade, releasing his cargo in the mountains near Long Tien. He was so sick of feeling as if all he was doing was stuffing rice in the bellies of the people of Laos, when there was no end to the insanity in sight. He didn't give a shit about communism. The heroin trade was marching on unstoppable. The menace, the real menace, was hunger and war lords, and a system glutted by bribery.

Razor looked over at him. "God bless the good ol' U.S. of A."

Jimmy looked at him, then headed toward home base. "Whatever the fuck you say."

"You don't love the U.S. of A.?"

"I just want to go home," Jimmy shouted over the noise of the engine.

They flew back to their air base, Jimmy sweating the whole way. He remembered when Chief asked him if he had steel balls. *When you don't have a lot to lose, you've got steel balls.* You just don't fucking care. He had loved Mai when he met Chief, but after she came to Saigon, after living together with little Tam, he—Jimmy Malone, from Hell's fucking Kitchen—began to glimpse something after the war. Something good.

They landed on a tiny airstrip, just some flattened grass.

Razor hounded him again. "Come on, Malone. You been in this country too long? Starting to forget how good it is in the U.S.A.?"

"Trust me, I haven't forgotten," Jimmy muttered. He started to climb out of the plane. Forget how good it was? He wanted to open a bar where the keg was always cold and there were no bargirls' babies crying upstairs.

"I think you have. Come on." Razor wore his hair as short as a marine fresh out of basic. "Come on...you forgettin' why we're here?"

Jimmy hopped out, and so did Razor, still flapping his gums.

"I hate you guys," Razor said, "getting all you can from Uncle Sam. Bet you sympathize with the flowerheads back home." He started toward Jimmy, head pressed forward like a bull.

Jimmy whirled around. "Get off my back. I don't care if this place is overrun with communists. Let the NVA take it all. Laos...'Nam. All of it. I don't give a fuck."

"Fuck a gook and that's what you get. You get your head all twisted by gook pussy."

Jimmy was on the guy immediately. He clocked him with a solid left to the jaw. Razor swung back, but Jimmy landed a right square on his nose and felt the cartilage crush beneath his fist.

Razor started screaming and swinging, blood spraying Jimmy in the face. But Jimmy didn't care. He swung until his arms hurt, and even as Chuck, a mechanic, and two other pilots pulled him off, he kept swinging.

Finally someone landed a solid hook to his face to snap him out of it. Jimmy shook off the punch, gasping for air.

He looked down on the ground at Razor, who appeared half dead. His face was just blood, like raw meat, and he wasn't conscious.

"Christ, Jimmy!" Chuck said, his Texas twang deep and baritone.

Jimmy stood over Razor. "You say something about my girl ever again and next time I'll kill you."

"He can't even fuckin' hear ya, Jimmy," Chuck said. The other two pilots just stared at him as if he had finally lost it.

"Then when he wakes up, you tell him. And the same goes for the rest of you. One word about Mai and I'll slit your throats."

Wiping the blood on his hands down the front of his shirt, Jimmy sauntered away. And when he was finally out of sight, out of earshot, then he allowed the shaking in his hands to show. And then, only then, had he allowed a small cry to escape from his throat.

After that, things were tense. Then Chief came looking for him. He said he'd pissed off "all the right people" in Washington.

"You have enemies, Jimmy."

"Enemies. How you guys can talk like that is beyond me. You don't know who the enemy is. You say it's people with slanty eyes, but you can't tell. You have no clue." Jimmy was convinced the war was going to be over soon. You can't win a war filling bellies with rice.

"No. I know who, and I'm telling you, it goes high up in the agency. I don't know what you did, but they're watching you."

At the time, he presumed it was because of what he'd done

to Razor. But since Tam disappeared, he wasn't sure anymore. Back in the States, he'd had a private detective friend of his follow the thread of Tam to the hospital the old priest had told him about. It seemed to check out—except the nurse on that floor couldn't describe Tam. She remembered her as thin, when Tam was chubby. On top of that, the private detective, who was really a cop who'd boozed his way out of the NYPD, said the nurse was skittish.

Jimmy didn't know what to think. Had they stashed Tam somewhere to make sure he stayed in line? He wanted out. He had his money, he'd risked his neck and now he wanted his girl. He wanted to go home. And he didn't want to have to watch for the shadows of war anymore. But something told him he would always have to. And he couldn't shake the feeling that it had something to do with Tam.

Chapter Twenty-Nine

"I'm your uncle Terry," he said. "Come in."

At first, Maggie wondered how he recognized them considering he hadn't seen them since they were kids, crying at their mother's funeral. But she assumed he didn't have too many Amer-Asian brothers and sisters land on his doorstep. She took a couple of steps into the house and he gave her a gentle hug, whispering, "You look just like Mai."

Bobby followed, and Maggie said, "This is my boyfriend, Bobby Gonzalez."

Uncle Terry shook Bobby's hand. "Nice to meet you."

Danny stepped into the foyer next.

"I'm not even going to ask if they look worse," Uncle Terry said ruefully.

"They don't," Danny muttered.

"This way," their uncle said, shutting and locking the door and setting the alarm, then leading the way to an immense den. There was a large fireplace, rich leather couches and plush Oriental rugs, and fourteen-foot ceilings. Bookcases rose from floor to ceiling, and Maggie noticed a rolling ladder against one of them, allowing someone to climb to the top shelves to retrieve a volume.

"Would you like a drink?" Their uncle gestured toward a small bar set into an antique hutch with cut-crystal decanters.

"I'll take a ginger ale if you have it," Maggie said.

"Coke or ginger ale," Bobby said.

Danny nodded toward a decanter. "Bourbon and soda."

Maggie watched as her uncle made the drinks. He took an ice bucket and said, "I'll be right back."

While he was gone, Danny looked at Maggie. "So we've had a rich fucking uncle all these years."

She smiled at him. "Appears so."

Bobby walked over to a bookshelf. "This guy seriously digs Milton."

"He's my specialty," Terry said as he reappeared with the ice bucket. "Are you familiar with him?"

"*Paradise Lost*, right?" Bobby asked.

Terrence smiled. He dropped cubes into their drinks with a pair of tongs and then made himself a scotch. "I feel a bit lost today myself. I got word your father...is dead."

"Who told you?" Maggie asked.

"Anonymous call. I tried to trace it, but the call came from a calling card."

He raised his glass. "I'm sorry. To Jimmy," he spoke softly.

They all lifted their glasses and sipped.

"Let's sit down," Terry gestured to the couches.

Maggie and Bobby moved to one, and sank down into the butter-soft leather. Danny sat in a big club chair. His eyes were at half-mast. Painkillers.

"So what do you know?" Terry asked.

Danny shook his head. "No. We don't play that game. You may be our uncle, but we don't know shit about you. So why don't you just tell us your piece of the puzzle and then we'll fill you in."

Terry looked down into his glass. "Fair enough."

Maggie reached over and held Bobby's hand. Terry looked so much like their father that it made it hard for her to look at him.

"Well, Mai lived with me when she first came to America. And I fell in love with her."

The comment hung in the air, and Maggie didn't breathe or move.

Terry looked up, his eyes moist. "She didn't return my feelings. She cared about me, but it was your father she loved. I knew she didn't love me." He was quiet for a moment. "But it was enough to have her living with me. We spent our evenings listening to music, one of the few things we could do because we had a hard time understanding each other sometimes."

He took a deep breath. "Tam was, according to your father, supposed to have arrived, too. But she didn't, and at first we thought it was a communication foul-up. Then we heard reports she was dead. That's what the priest who got her papers together said."

Maggie felt a stabbing pain in her chest. She couldn't have traveled this far to lose her father and her sister in one fell swoop. "Dead," she managed to let out.

He nodded. "We didn't believe it, though. But we had no clues. Eventually, your father returned from Vietnam. Laos.

They said he nearly killed a man, that it had all gotten to him. Vietnam fell to the NVA. The general the CIA was backing fled Laos… We were losing all our interests in Asia. So they sent Jimmy home. When he got here, well…" He smiled.

"What?" Danny asked.

"We shared a room growing up. We knew each other better than anyone. After your uncle Michael died, it was just us two. We had always understood each other, even though our lives took different paths. So when he got here, he could tell."

"Tell what?" Danny asked.

"That he loved Mom," Maggie said. Leave it to men to be so dense about affairs of the heart.

Terry continued. "He packed her up and told me that if I ever came near her, he'd kill me. You know, I never would have tried to come between them. I did love her, but I never wished for him not to come back. I didn't. She had me believing in karma. I couldn't wish anything but good."

He gave a nervous laugh. "She left me one of her Buddha statues. She gave it to me. I keep it on my nightstand."

Maggie looked at her uncle. His hair was streaked with gray, but he had very few wrinkles, and his eyes were the same color as her father's.

"I tried to move on with my life. I lived in a different house then. Smaller." He smiled sheepishly. "College presidents need to show off a bit. The alumni like it. Anyway, it was a smaller home, but I still rattled around without her. I immersed myself in my work. And I would call from time to time. Then one day your father phoned me and told me she had committed suicide." His voice grew shaky, and he cleared his throat a couple of times.

Maggie looked at Bobby. She could feel the tension in his legs as her hand rested on his thigh.

"I went down for the funeral. Your father was a man destroyed. But in the midst of that, he forgave me. He knew I was probably the only other man alive who knew what it was like to lose her."

"I remember you being there," Maggie said softly. "I remember you holding me on your lap."

He looked away. "It was a closed-casket funeral. I never even got to look at her again. Your father and I promised to stay in touch. And then he found the film."

Chapter Thirty

Hell's kitchen, October 1986

Jimmy stared at the ceiling of his Hell's Kitchen apartment and tried to conjure an image of Mai lying next to him. He shut his eyes, hoping she would come to him, in his mind, like a ghost.

Her smile was always enigmatic, slightly sad. Her eyes looked not at him but into him. One war, oceans and continents of separation, nightmares for both of them, two kids—adorable but exhausting—in two years, and in the end, it was him not being able to save her that killed her. Not being able to save her from her sadness.

In his mind, he could picture her, but it was always for just a fraction of a second. As soon as he had it, the image would disintegrate to the morgue, her body so bloated that he, who had seen napalm victims, heaved until only bile came up. From there, his mind would spin backward until he could envision her at the East River, about to jump in. He would see himself running to save her, and always, she would turn her head, smile, and jump, and then the entire mosaic of painful images would start all over again.

At first they'd thought she was just missing. Jimmy had figured she had gone to Chinatown. She liked shopping for her Buddhas and lucky cats. But eventually, the East River gave Mai up.

Sweating, he sat up in bed. Without her there, it was hopeless trying to sleep. He'd have put a bullet in his own head if it weren't for Danny and Maggie.

Climbing out of bed, he pulled on a T-shirt and left his bedroom to go check on the kids. They shared a bedroom. He cracked the door open and peeked in.

Both kids looked nothing like him. They were all Mai, all beautiful Mai. Danny slept on his back, hand clutching a Buddha, rosary beads strung around the post of his bed. When Jimmy told him Mai had gone to heaven, the kid had been all confused. Buddhists don't have a heaven, so Jimmy struggled to decide which fairy tale to tell him. He finally settled on the idea that Mai had, indeed, covered both her bases. She was waiting in heaven until the perfect rebirth could be found.

He squinted over at Maggie. She was awake, lying on her side. He imagined Tam might look like Maggie if she was alive. If she was alive, which at this point, he doubted.

He swung the door open wider. "Hey, bright eyes," he whispered. "Can't sleep?"

"Uh-uh."

"Me neither. Come on." He gestured for her to come out into the living room.

Maggie climbed out of bed, her skinny little body encased in pink silk pajamas. She slid on fluffy pink slippers and followed Jimmy.

"Hungry?" he asked her, turning on the kitchen light. Lately, this had been their ritual. Ice cream at 2:00 a.m. He'd hired a cousin of his to close the bar some nights so he could be home more. He worked long hours opening and cleaning the place while they were at school. He'd come up and help them with their homework and would make dinner, tuck them in, and then the high-school senior who lived one floor up would sit there and eat his food, talk on his phone and watch his TV until late while they slept. The sitter would fall asleep on the couch, he'd come up, pay her and then lie awake. He'd eventually check on Maggie, eat ice cream and sleep a scant couple of hours before doing the same thing all over again.

"I'm a little hungry," Maggie said.

He made her a small dish of chocolate ice cream, and served himself a heaping portion of heavenly hash. They sat, side by side at the breakfast counter, eating the cold treat. It was the only thing that soothed his heart, watching Maggie eat, her eyes half-sleepy. Or tossing Danny high into the air, even though Danny was getting way too big for that.

Con came by on weekends. A brother to the end, he helped Jimmy with the kids and the bar. And when Jimmy told him he would never love another woman, never get over it, and would grieve until the day he died, Con never said, "Time will heal it." He didn't argue with him. Con knew.

"Can we talk to Buddha?" Maggie asked.

"Hmm?"

"I miss it. Mama used to make us talk to him every day. But I don't like to talk to him in front of Cara."

The babysitter was nice, but Cara's priorities were Doritos and gossip. Jimmy didn't even think she knew who Buddha was.

"Sure, bright eyes."

He lifted her from the bar stool and the two of them walked over to the altar in the corner of the living room. Maggie took a jasmine incense stick and lit it expertly with a Bic lighter. Good thing the kid's not a pyro, Jimmy mused.

Maggie bowed and then she whispered, "Dear Buddha, please send my ma to a good rebirth. And please, if you can, make her come to be with us. She can be a cat or a mouse. Or a person. Or anything. Just tell her to let us know. And please tell Jesus I said hello. And please help my daddy. He is very tired. And please help Danny to not cry so much. Thank you. You are very austicious."

"That's *auspicious*," Jimmy said as he suppressed a grin, even as he felt his throat constrict.

"Auspicious."

She looked up at him. "I can sleep now."

Jimmy lifted her up, and she buried her head into his neck and nuzzled him. He inhaled the scent of Johnson & Johnson baby shampoo. *God, Mai. Why?*

He carried Maggie back to her bed, tucked her blanket up to her chin and whispered, "Good night." He kissed each cheek, and then did an Eskimo kiss, and then, finally, a butterfly kiss on each eye. She sighed and snuggled down.

Jimmy shut the door and stood still for a minute. He could hear Chief asking him if he had steel balls, if he was as tough as everyone said he was. Jesus, but this was tougher. Those kids. Alone.

He looked over at the Buddha altar. Suddenly, he was angry. At Buddha, at a God he no longer believed in, at the war, at Chief, at everything. He strode over to the altar and lifted up the little cabinet that housed Buddha.

"Fuck you," he said to the statue. "You like that? Huh? Fuck you. Goddamnit." He knew he was losing it. "I'm sorry, Mai," he said. This was her altar. He didn't want to ruin it. So he went to put the cabinet back and set the statue neatly within it.

"What the fuck?" Jimmy's hand felt a small nail on the bottom of the cabinet. Taking the Buddha out gently, he put it on the table. He turned the cabinet completely upside down. It had a false bottom.

Jimmy opened it. Inside was an object wrapped in several red silk scarves. A Santeria priest who'd read Mai's cards once had told her red was for protection. Jimmy pulled whatever it was out and set the cabinet on the table. He untied the scarves one at a time.

And there, nestled in the middle, was a reel of film. Jimmy turned on the lamp in the corner. It was the brightest lamp. He took off the lamp shade and unspooled some of the film.

"Jesus Christ," he said to no one, to Mai, to Buddha, to whoever would listen at three a.m. in that apartment. He leaned his head closer to the film, seeing death unfold in tiny images. And in that instant, he knew Mai hadn't jumped. She had been pushed.

Chapter Thirty-One

Maggie looked at Terry. "I knelt at that altar a hundred times. A thousand times."

He nodded. "I know." He sipped his drink and rubbed his eyes. "This looks like it's shaping up to be a long night. I've got a lot more ground to cover. Are you all hungry? I'm being a terrible host, a terrible uncle. I could fix you dinner. You'll stay the night, right?" When they didn't respond, he added, "It's not like I don't have the room."

Maggie exchanged glances with Danny, who blinked at her slowly, a subtle okay. She smiled at her uncle. "We won't be any trouble. We can order takeout."

"Come on," he said and smiled back at her. "I'm a fabulous cook, I just rarely have the opportunity to put my skills to use. I can tell you the rest of the story, and you can fill me in on your lives."

He stood and motioned for them to follow him to the kitchen. When he flicked on the lights, Maggie was in awe. The kitchen was cavernous, a giant island in the center of it,

with a grill, sink and plenty of counter space. All the cabinets were a rich cherrywood with pewter knobs. The coun-
tertops were granite and marble, and the restaurant-quality
appliances were all recessed into the cabinets and disguised
with wood. Shining stainless steel pots hung from a suspended rack, and wine bottles filled several wrought-iron
structures that looked like modern sculptures. Fresh vegetables filled baskets, colorful fruits filled bowls.

"All this and you just cook for yourself?" Maggie asked.

"Afraid so. How does pasta with some olive oil, basil and
some fresh tomatoes sound? Some salad? Bread?"

"Sounds heavenly," Maggie said, realizing she was hungry
for more than Cheez-Its from gas stations.

"Sit, please." He nodded toward high-backed stools along
the island. "I'll open a nice red wine, and we'll let it breathe
while I cook."

Maggie, Danny and Bobby watched as he busied himself
with opening the wine and gathering cloves of garlic, which
he began cutting on a wooden board.

"Bobby, what do you do?" Terry asked.

"You're the first person I've met in the last two days who
didn't guess straight off. I'm a cop. A detective."

Terry chuckled. "I thought so."

Bobby grinned.

Terry looked at him. "Did you bring guns with you?"

Bobby nodded.

"I'm not a man who believes in violence, but in this
case, good."

"What did my father do after he found the film?" Maggie pressed.

Terry moved to the sink and filled a large pot with water, then switched on a flame on the gas stove. He chopped plum tomatoes and basil as he answered.

"Well, your father had always assumed it was his own past that doomed Tam. He thought somehow, when things didn't add up, that it was payback for asking the wrong questions, seeing too much, a payload of heroin. He didn't know. After he found the film, he couldn't understand why Mai didn't tell him about the massacre. He thought the village was lost in battle, not in outright slaughter. But that was when we all thought Tam was her sister, not her daughter. We didn't understand. Your father, Con, Hop…me… We would look at the film, we would analyze it all, and we knew it was there, right in front of us. But we couldn't see it."

"See what?" Danny asked.

Terry looked up. "We didn't know. We didn't know what we were chasing. We knew that there was a massacre. We knew she had the film. That Tam was missing or dead. But none of it made sense. We kept looking for a connection to Air America. To heroin. To Vang Pao, maybe."

"Who's he?" Maggie asked.

"Military leader of the Hmong in Laos. He was involved in the heroin trade. See, we kept looking for links to the agency, and meanwhile the keys were right there, if only we would have looked. Really looked."

"I don't understand," Maggie said.

Terry put the tomatoes into a sauté pan. He pulled down four wineglasses.

"We don't drink," Bobby said. "Maggie and I. We don't drink."

"I'm sorry." He put two of the glasses back but didn't ask. "When your father finally saw the tape, it was dark and confusing. You've seen it, right?"

They all nodded.

"Then you know there's only one short point when Calhoun turns and is recognizable. And we couldn't fathom, if Calhoun was behind it, that he would have known, could have known, who Mai was or what she had on film. If he knew she had filmed it, he would have killed her right then and there."

He pulled down some plates. "When Mai came here, she had no way of knowing Calhoun was anything but a soldier. She couldn't have known about his family connections. Couldn't have known anything about him."

Maggie watched as her uncle started cooking, adding some salt to the water on the stove.

"But back in Vietnam, Con and Hop had tipped their hand. They had gone to Calhoun for help to find Mai and Tam after the massacre. He at least knew Mai was a witness. And that maybe she hadn't died because she had probably hidden in the spot they had built for her. Then, when Calhoun saw the photo of Mai and Tam that Con showed him, it couldn't have been too hard to put two and two together."

"Two and two?" Danny asked as he downed the last of his bourbon.

"What we never saw in Tam. That she was part white. Your father never saw it. I mean, you two look so much like Mai and very little like your father. But Calhoun, he saw it. And he must have recognized Mai as the girl he once raped. We're sure of it."

He poured glasses of red wine for himself and Danny.

"So why didn't Dad just…handle it the way Dad would? Go after Calhoun. Kill him. Whatever. You know Daddy," Maggie said.

Terry smiled sadly. "You know, revenge consumed your father, but he was willing to wait. He was willing to wait until that precise moment when he could bring total devastation to the bastard. Until he had Tam, he wasn't willing to confront Calhoun. As long as he could find Tam, he was willing to wait. And in the meantime, he would go off on these…missions. Finding surviving members of Calhoun's platoon that massacred the village."

"How many of them are left?" Bobby asked, leaning over the counter.

"There were five." He prepared salad, pulling more tomatoes from the basket on the island.

"That's it?" Danny asked, sipping his wine. Maggie saw him clench and unclench his jaw, and she longed to somehow make it all better.

"Calhoun was eventually moved to a more administrative position because of his father. He served out the rest of his tour in a safer situation. But the rest of his buddies lost a battle for a strategic hill. Most of them died in combat. Five made it back to America. Plus Calhoun."

"And?" Maggie was holding her breath, feeling as if the massive kitchen were closing in on her.

He dropped pasta into the boiling water.

"One committed suicide three years after he came home. Stuck a gun in his mouth. One died of a drug overdose. That left three. Another was murdered."

"Christ," said Bobby. "Did they ever solve it?"

"No. It was done execution style, though."

"That leaves two witnesses," Bobby said.

Terry nodded. "There's a tape in my safe upstairs that your father made. It's an interview with one of those two surviving members. It's damning. Now, I don't know that it's admissible because your father was off camera aiming a gun at the guy's head, but I've no doubt it's the truth. After the interview, that surviving soldier died of pancreatic cancer maybe four months later."

"Which leaves one," Danny said.

"Which leaves one." Terry sighed. "Michael Flynn. And he's off the grid."

Bobby shook his head. "More guys off the grid. Jesus."

"But Jimmy found him. Six months ago. I know where he is."

"Oh my God." Maggie felt hope rising. "Then he might know where Tam is. Or he can help us nail Calhoun. Make Calhoun tell us where she is."

Terry was silent. He poured the spaghetti and water through a colander and began serving the food. Maggie watched him. His expression had turned grim.

"Come on, let's all sit down." They moved over to the cherrywood dining table. Terry turned on the frosted-glass chandelier over the island and used the dimmer to soften the lighting. He brought over the silverware, bread and salad.

They each sat down.

"Tam," Maggie said. "Does Flynn know where Tam is?"

"No," Terry said, sinking his head into his hands. "I do."

Chapter Thirty-Two

Hell's Kitchen, April 1985

Mai never fully mastered reading English, but she spoke it well, if heavily accented. Nonetheless, she never stopped educating herself. One of her greatest fears was that one day her children would think she was stupid. They would advance in their American education and she had never even gone to formal school.

To make sure this never happened, Mai would take their schoolbooks out of their backpacks each night, while Jimmy was still working and the children were asleep. Then she would read and study the lessons for the next day, so she was certain she could answer any question they might have, even in math, which she hated.

But this was not enough. So Mai decided that each Sunday she would read the *New York Times*. And this was difficult. It would take her all week to get through most of the articles, and she would skip anything having to do with Wall

Street. She knew Jimmy believed in cash. He hid mountains of it in the wall of the bathroom, behind some loose tiles. And he hid cash in shoe boxes. They had a bank account, but it didn't reflect how much money they had. Jimmy didn't trust the government or the IRS, and Mai knew cash was what had bought her way to the United States, so cash she trusted. Not the stock market.

So, other than any Wall Street articles, she made her way through the *Times*. One Tuesday night, she saw that the Sunday magazine had done an article on Vietnam relations ten years after the fall of Saigon. She turned to it and began reading. The reporters interviewed several former soldiers, including one man from a politically prominent family from Indiana.

Mai turned the page. Her reaction was physical. She began to tremble, unable even to hold her hands still. Her eyes filled with tears until she couldn't see. Her vision was blurry, but there he was. The devil. Standing in his office, in front of an American flag. He wore a dark blue suit, but his eyes were the same. And peeking up from beneath his collar was the burn.

Mai bolted from the table to the bathroom and locked the door. Then she allowed herself to collapse to the floor, certain she was safe from the eyes of her children if they awoke. She didn't want to frighten them. Curled into a fetal position, she cried.

When she'd been pregnant with Danny, she'd tried not to think about him being taken from her someday. When he was born, she'd never let him out of her sight. Then came Maggie. Mai's sweet babies and her brave Jimmy gave her a reason to live again, but in her heart, she never let go of the idea that one day she would be reunited with Tam.

The sobs came from a place Mai had shut off from the rest of herself. In that place, like a river choked with reeds, were her mother, the massacre, her wicked *Tante*, the night the burned man had raped her. Mai cried on the floor of the bathroom until she felt the choked-off place was empty.

Now she had a name. Calhoun. And a place. Indiana. She would find that on a map. And she would find out everything she could about him. She would find Tam, because in her mind, he'd taken her. She wasn't sure why she thought that, but she did.

Mai rose from the bathroom floor and washed her face. She peered into the mirror. She had changed little. Now she sometimes wore mascara or a little lipstick, but her hair was still to her waist, silky and shiny, her cheekbones still very high, her eyes still black. She had changed little, yet changed much. She was strong like a soldier.

Mai went out to her Buddha altar and prayed. The next day, while the children were in school, she traveled to Chinatown and searched for a *gao*. She found one, and the man who sold it to her said the symbol on its front was for perseverance.

When Mai got home, she went to the little porcelain box in which she stored all of the many fortune-cookie slips she kept for good luck. She found one that read *You are faithful and will persevere.* Jimmy had told her what *perseverance* meant. She turned the slip over and then in careful strokes of Vietnamese lettering, she wrote *Calhoun, give back our daughter.*

Mai rolled the piece of paper so tightly and small that it could fit in the *gao* box locket. She opened the secret door in back of the locket and put the paper in there. The *gao* was for prayers, and this was hers. *Give her back.*

Mai shut the *gao* and strung it on a black silk cord, which she then wore around her neck. She swore to herself that until Calhoun gave Tam back, she would never take it off.

Chapter Thirty-Three

Danny watched as Terry collected himself. Danny wasn't sure that he wanted to hear what came next. Somehow losing his father would be somewhat bearable if Tam was alive, but if she wasn't, then what the hell had their mother suffered for?

As a Buddhist covering her bases, Mai had taught that suffering was inevitable, but Danny thought this much suffering was too much. Too much for him, too much for Maggie.

Terry continued, "At your mother's funeral, I was devastated. Your father and I...we were brothers again. And I was there to try to support him, but inside, I was dying, too. I tried to be strong for him and for you all."

He looked up at them. "I placed her on a pedestal. She was so pure of heart. Anyway, your father and I were in your apartment after the funeral. We were sitting there, numb. 'Now what?' Jimmy kept asking. Two kids to raise and no Mai, the love of his life. We sat there, the two of us, in the dark. I think we had a candle or two burning, but we were just sitting there in silence. I looked over at her altar. Jimmy said what a lot of good her religion did her.

"I got up and walked over to it. Jimmy came up next to me, and we just stood there looking at the Buddha. Then Jimmy reached over and removed Mai's *gao* from the Buddha's neck."

"Her what?" Bobby asked. None of them were eating. They were all listening to Terry so intently.

"A *gao* box. A locket," Terry said. "But if you didn't know it was a locket, you might not recognize it as such. It looked like a silver box and had a symbol on the front. Jimmy said she always wore it. So we thought she took it off because she was planning on committing suicide. But she actually left it for us."

"As a clue?" Maggie asked.

Terry nodded. "Selfishly, I wanted something of hers to take home with me. I lifted it up and looked at it, and I started crying. I just fell apart. Your father told me to take the necklace. I stuck it in my pocket and brought it home with me to Boston, and I hung it from my bedside lamp. I would look at it every night, every morning, but…I don't know, I didn't touch it or handle it. It was like this sacred thing to me. I would just look at it."

Danny was still waiting to hear what this had to do with Tam, but Terry had obviously waited a long time to tell them the story of Mai as he knew it, so Danny tried to be patient.

"After he found the film, we talked a lot, your father and I. Banging our heads against the wall. We didn't know who the soldier was. And one night, I have no idea why, I took the *gao* and held it, and I talked to her. To Mai. I asked her to tell me what she wanted me to do. And I fingered the box and realized it opened. And I unrolled a fortune."

"Like from a cookie?" Bobby asked.

"Yeah. So I unrolled it, and on the front was a fortune-cookie message about perseverance. On the back was her writing, in Vietnamese."

"What did it say?" Danny asked.

"I got a translator at the university to tell me. *Calhoun, give back our daughter.* It was the piece we were missing, what we hadn't seen, like blind men stumbling. Now more of it started to make sense. Jimmy remembered her becoming very distraught over an article in the *Times.* He found the article. Calhoun was in it."

"So how did he feel when he found out Tam was her daughter and not her sister?" Danny asked.

"Terrible. I mean, he knew, in an instant, it was a rape. Some things he left private, but I presume maybe she…you know, had told him something or hinted about a rape. Between them, in their love life. So he knew. He just wished she had told him. And then he felt he now knew for sure that Calhoun was behind Tam's disappearance."

"So where is our sister?" Danny asked.

"She was under our noses the whole time. Calhoun has a wife and two kids. The trophy wife. As he started moving into the national stage, we knew he had a first marriage and a daughter, Julie. The first wife died of breast cancer. The daughter was in academia. But because this new wife is such a politico, well, no one ever even talks about the first marriage and daughter except as a minor footnote. And finally, as we looked deeper into his past, we found out that Julie was Vietnamese. She's adopted. Dr. Julie Calhoun, a professor at Georgetown in D.C., is your half sister. She's Tam."

"She's alive," Maggie whispered.

"Thank God," Danny said, feeling his voice choke a little. "But the fucking evil prick adopted the child of his own rape? Brought her home to his wife? Christ."

"She has no idea?" Maggie asked.

Terry shook his head. "No. Calhoun's father is still a wily SOB. I don't know whether it's him pulling all the strings, or just Calhoun, or both. Or even Calhoun's wife. They all have big-time connections. I only know your father is dead, we have the film, we know where Flynn is, and we can try to get to him before they do. But in the end, it's Tam you want. I mean, you can bring this bastard down, and I would take him down hard, but you want to be able to reach Tam."

Danny had no intention of taking Calhoun down. He was going to kill him in cold blood. He owed his mother and father that. Take him down? No. But he had time for that. He wanted to go to his sister. His other sister. The ghost sister of their childhood. He wanted to tell her about the way their mother had kept her secrets and had never stopped hoping to find her.

"What does she teach?" Bobby asked.

Terry started laughing.

"What?" Maggie asked.

"What does karma tell you? The cycle goes round and round, unbroken, over and over. Your sister teaches comparative religion and eastern philosophy."

Suddenly, the air felt lighter to Danny. That was karmic justice, really, Danny thought. The four of them started to eat, grateful for the story of Mai from their uncle, the piece of the puzzle that was out there now.

"Why did it take so long to find her?" Maggie asked.

"Well, we had Calhoun's name but Tam was still a single child lost during Operation Babylift. We went back to the hospital where she disappeared. We interviewed the two adoption volunteers on the plane. We even tracked down some of the Babylift kids—now grown—to ask them. But she was like a needle in a haystack. Your father didn't want to confront Calhoun directly, tip his hand too early, so he was off finding all the guys from Calhoun's platoon. He also wanted you to be safe. If he tipped off that he knew too much, you might have been hurt." Terry looked at Danny's face. "I can see we were right about that. Anyway, we kept digging and digging until we found her. Maybe a year or two ago. Then we had the information, but we still weren't sure what to do with it. Take Calhoun down, but at what cost to Tam?"

Terry asked them about their lives. Maggie told him about the bar.

"The Twilight's trendy now?" He laughed. "I remember the days when you were taking your life in your hands to go in there."

"Funny how things go round and round," Maggie said. "Maybe even the Twilight has karma."

They continued eating. When dinner was done, Danny sipped his wine. "Well, I guess we head to D.C. tomorrow."

"We can't thank you enough for this, Uncle Terry. We promise to keep in touch now," Maggie added and she leaned over to pat her uncle's hand.

"But I'm coming with you."

"No way," Danny said. It was bad enough that when the time came to put a bullet into Calhoun, he'd have to deal with Bobby. But Terry, too? No. Maggie understood the way justice was sometimes meted out. But Terry would never understand.

"I need to. Besides, you need me if you're going to find Mike Flynn."

"Look, Terry, we appreciate all you've done for us," Danny said, "but my battered face was courtesy of guys who seemed agency or Secret Service to me. Either that or former ones on somebody's payroll. We came here because Hop's bar is blown to smithereens, and we can't get hold of Con. We don't know if we're gonna come out the other side of this alive. I'm not happy Maggie's in this, but we don't need anyone else getting hurt."

Terry looked at Danny. "I know you're a tough guy. I know who my brother was. But I was raised in Hell's Kitchen, too. My brains may have gotten me out of there, but I can handle myself."

"Sorry, Terry," Danny said. "But you've been living the life a little too long. Expensive wine, fancy foods, antiques. You may think you remember Hell's Kitchen, but you don't."

"Don't belittle me. I've been behind the scenes with your father every inch of finding Tam. I hold the key to bringing Calhoun down. If we have Mike Flynn and the film, then we have congressional hearings, the FBI, *60 Minutes.*"

"*60 Minutes?*" Danny snapped. "The same guys who squashed the tobacco-company story? Don't tell me you're putting your faith in the fucking media! Jesus Christ, you've been out of Hell's Kitchen too long. You're naive, Terry." He whipped the Glock out of his waistband. "This is what I put my faith in." He waved the weapon in the air.

Terry half rose, putting out his hands. "Danny, I'm just saying there's a way to play this. I'm coming."

"You don't have the right to come. She was our mother."

Terry suddenly pushed back from the table and got up. They watched as he stormed from the room. Maggie scolded Danny. "You're being too hard on him. Without him, we wouldn't even know where she is."

"I'm being honest. Bobby, you see he shouldn't come, right?"

Bobby nodded. "Just from the perspective of wanting as few people to get hurt as possible. We need to keep this as small as we can."

Terry came back into the room, clutching a black cord, a silver locket dangling from it. "*This* gives me the right. She may not have loved me the way she loved your father, but she lived with me, and she trusted me. She used to call me sometimes, when Jimmy would go off on his adventures, whatever they were, and she was worried and afraid. I was the one she told when she might be pregnant with you, Danny. I was her friend and her brother-in-law, and they killed her and my brother, and *that* gives me the right."

Maggie looked at Danny pleadingly, and he couldn't say no to her. It was that simple.

"Fine." Terry could be there, Danny thought. It still wouldn't matter. Senator Calhoun was going to get his karmic comeuppance. He was going to go to his rebirth as a maggot, or he was going to hell. Either way, the journey would be unpleasant.

Chapter Thirty-Four

September 1985

Mai decided she had waited long enough to see her child. She tried to be patient. She had prayed, and she had burned incense. She had trekked to St. Patrick's Cathedral, and she had even gone to a synagogue. Finally, she decided she had been patient long enough. So she called up the state senator's office and spoke to a secretary. She told her she had a message. She made the woman read it back to her two times.

"I have some information about an incident in Vietnam. It had to do with his daughter. He'll know what that means." Mai left her number.

Part of her knew that she was playing a dangerous game, and she wanted to tell Jimmy everything. But she couldn't, for the simple reason that Jimmy would kill Calhoun, and she did not want his karma to be tainted. She had been with Jimmy a while now, and she worked on him gently. When he was around her, he was peaceful. But she knew when he left their apartment, he was not so peaceful.

Three days later, while the children were at school, a man called the apartment. He said he was arranging for a meeting. She was to come to a place on the East River—a warehouse—bring her information, and she would get whatever it was she wanted in two days' time.

Mai was both elated and frightened. Jimmy always warned her about things that were too good to be true. Living with him, she'd learned he valued loyalty above all else, and he had a great ability to see things only for good or bad. The world of Jimmy Malone had little gray and most people had to earn his trust. She tried to think like him, but it was hard. All she could think about was getting Tam back.

The night before her scheduled meeting, Mai and Jimmy made love. She imagined that maybe they had even made a baby. Then they would have four children. As he held her in the darkness of their room, she whispered, "I love you."

"I love you, too, Mai."

"I think, no matter what, we will be together for many lifetimes."

"I hope so," he said, kissing the top of her head as she nestled against him.

Usually, she fell asleep first, but this night, she forced her eyes to stay open. Then, when she heard Jimmy's breath get heavy with the rhythm of sleep, she slid from bed and got the film from inside a shoe box shoved far back on the top shelf of the closet. She went to her altar. Wrapping the film in many scarves, she hid it there. She was no fool—Jimmy had taught her always to have a backup plan, always to be prepared for any eventuality. To her, he was like Lao-tzu. As versed as she was in the peace of Buddha, he knew the art of war. She would not go to the meeting with the film she planned to use against Calhoun. When they produced Tam, she would let him have the film she took of the massacre, of him. She would give him his future in exchange for her child.

The next day, she kissed her children goodbye. She gave them extra kisses, including an Eskimo kiss, which Jimmy had taught her how to do. It always made Maggie giggle. She cooked Jimmy a fried egg on noodles and she brewed him some coffee. After kissing her goodbye, Jimmy went down to the bar. She dressed and got ready to go. Just as she was about to leave, she thought of the horrible possibility that these men would not be honorable, and Jimmy would not know where she was. She took off the *gao* she wore and left it at the altar, trusting he would eventually be able to figure it out, finding the film and the *gao* together.

Then she went to the meeting, taking the subway and walking. She stood outside the warehouse address. The neighborhood was, as Jimmy would say, questionable. A four-door black car pulled up. Three men in suits got out. None of them was Calhoun.

"Where is he?" she asked. Her voice was not weak or quavering. She had waited a long, long time for her daughter, and she was firm and resolute that today, an auspicious day, she would get her back no matter what.

"Where is the information?" one of the men asked. He put one hand on his hip, revealing a gun in a holster. He had black hair cut very close to his head. Jimmy had taught her shiny shoes and short hair often meant the police.

"I have a film to exchange for Tam."

"Where is it?"

"I'm not telling." She crossed her arms, hoping that made her look tough.

He withdrew the gun. "Seems we're at a bit of an impasse. We want the film, Mrs. Malone."

Shocked that they knew her name, Mai scrambled. They knew everything. "Maybe I have no film. Maybe I just say that to get my daughter."

"I don't think so."

Behind Mai was the East River. She took several steps backward. The wind whipped her hair around her face.

"Tell us where the film is and what's on it."

"I want my daughter."

The three men, each very large, walked toward her. Mai realized she had made a terrible mistake. But the one very smart thing she had done was hiding the film.

"Where is the film?"

"I mail it to my friend for safekeeping."

"What friend?"

"Han. She live in Vietnam."

Mai picked a name that was impossible to trace. Han could be any woman in Vietnam.

"Last name? Address?"

Mai took another step backward. "Don't come near me. I jump."

"You won't jump, Mrs. Malone. When did you mail the film?"

"I mail it one year ago. For safekeeping." Mai knew that if they checked, they would find out that she and Jimmy kept no safety deposit boxes, so deep was his mistrust of banks and government. It would be just like Jimmy Malone—or his wife—to keep money in the bathroom wall and to mail a film to a trusted friend.

"We want the film, that's all we want."

Jimmy told Mai stories of men who had been tortured. He said Uncle Sam was very creative in his methods. She decided she would prefer the water. She turned and looked down.

"Mrs. Malone," one of the men said in a soothing voice as he drew his gun. "You don't want to do that." She heard the click of a gun's safety.

Mai heard them starting toward her, their footsteps clattering on the pavement. "Forgive me," she whispered, and Mai Malone, her thin body lithe and graceful, arms stretched wide, stepped off the pier and into the swirling ebony waters below her.

Chapter Thirty-Five

The next day, after a restless night in one of Terry's guest rooms, Bobby drove to D.C. with Maggie beside him. They had decided to take Terry's Cadillac to Washington. "Might as well have a smooth ride," Danny had said as he looked the car over in the garage. Terry and Danny rode in the back, and Bobby noticed Danny was tapering off the painkillers, but he was also becoming more on edge.

Bobby liked Maggie's uncle. He seemed very intelligent, and considering what kind of a mess they were in, intelligence was an asset. Terry had formulated the plan. He'd called Dr. Julie Calhoun in his role as the president of Manchester University, to see if she was available to meet him for dinner to discuss her giving a special lecture at his university. He hadn't been able to reach her but had left word with both her departmental secretary and also on her voice mail, leaving his cell-phone number.

They decided to stay at a visible hotel where it was less

likely anyone would try something. They booked a suite at the Washington Hilton using Terry's name.

When they checked in, Bobby and Maggie took one room in the suite, and Danny and Terry took the other, with a living room between them. In their room, Bobby set down their bags and said, "I'm going to take a shower. Want to come?"

She smiled at him. "Sure. Maybe it will help me relax."

They undressed, and Bobby walked into the bathroom and started the shower, turning the temperature to very hot, wanting the steam and heat to soften the knots in his shoulders and neck.

He stepped into the shower and she followed. "What if my sister doesn't want to know the truth? What if she doesn't even want to know who her mother was?"

Bobby opened a small hotel bottle of shower gel that smelled of ginger and mint, and started soaping Maggie's shoulders.

"The thing with truth, Maggie, is you can only speak it. What other people choose to do with it is out of your control. It's like AA. People can come to meetings and hear the truth about alcoholism, but they won't get well until they want to. They will do what they want with the message they hear.

"But after all this, if we can't get her to listen to us, then it was all for nothing. My mother died to find her. So did my father. Then they died for nothing."

"Not for nothing. So that she has a choice."

Maggie looked up at him. She opened a shampoo bottle and began lathering. Bobby found his hands traveling down her back. He kissed her in the steam. He was struggling in all this to find his bearings.

He was a cop. And he had no idea what Danny would do when he finally confronted Calhoun—because Bobby knew that was exactly where this was going to go. They kept calling it end game. Checkmate. Whatever you wanted to name it, they were all barreling toward Calhoun in one way or the other. He could watch his own life go up in flames for Maggie, for Tam, for this truth that needed telling. He was swept as if by a current, and he wasn't sure if he still remembered how to swim.

Even being a cop aside, he had found a spiritual center in AA. He had no idea how he felt about some sort of karmic comeuppance for Calhoun.

Maggie slid against him, her breasts soapy against his chest and belly. "I need you," she whispered.

They continued kissing in the shower until their fingers were wrinkled. Finally, reluctantly, he turned off the water and grabbed two towels.

As he dried her body, she turned away from him and said, "Please make me a promise. Don't let Danny kill him. Calhoun deserves it, but if I have to spend the rest of my life visiting Danny in prison, I'll die. My heart already feels half-dead with all this. Please, Bobby?"

He rubbed the towel down her back. "I can try, Maggie, but your brother doesn't strike me as somebody who's ever listened to anyone his whole life, except maybe you. I can tell that his sun rises and sets with you."

"But you'll try. You'll try, right?" She turned and looked up at him, her damp hair clinging to her cheeks.

"I'll try," Bobby said. But even as he made the promise, he felt like a pitiful liar.

They finished drying off and got dressed. It was late and the long drive from Boston had made them very tired. Suddenly, there was a knock from the adjoining living room door.

"Yeah?" Maggie opened the door. It was Terry.

"She called. Your sister is on her way over here. We're to meet her in the hotel bar. Come on."

Bobby looked at Maggie, whose face registered abject terror. When Terry turned around, Bobby took Maggie by the hand. "Wherever your mother is, Maggie, this is her moment. It will be fine."

He squeezed her hand, and the two of them went into the living-room area. Terry opened the door to the suite. "Here we go. For Mai."

"For Mom," Maggie said. She looked over at Danny. Bobby saw that he was alert. Still no painkillers. He was hurting, Bobby could tell, but at least he was trying to keep his shit together to meet Tam.

Julie Calhoun.

The ghost child. The invisible girl of Maggie's past.

Chapter Thirty-Six

Maggie felt a combination of dread and excitement as they sat at a small table in the bar of the Hilton waiting for Tam. The bar was filled with businessmen and tourists. The four of them huddled together, speaking in whispers, discussing how they would present the information to her. Maggie wondered if Tam had ever dreamed of having a sister or a brother.

About thirty minutes later, a woman walked into the bar.

"She's your twin," Terry said, his mouth dropping open slightly.

Julie Calhoun had the same long, dark hair as Maggie, and the same almond-shaped eyes and slightly heart-shaped face. Her build, even to the long, tapered fingers, was just like Maggie's. She was wearing black pants and a simple black turtleneck. Around her neck was a strand of jade beads.

Terry stood up and waved. Julie smiled and approached.

"Terrence Malone," he said and stuck out his hand. "Please sit down." He gestured at an empty seat they'd left for her.

"Thank you," she smiled, but looked a little puzzled by the presence of three extra people.

As they had discussed, he was direct right away rather than prolonging things.

"Dr. Calhoun—"

"Please, call me Julie."

"Julie, then. I'm afraid I've brought you here under false pretenses."

Maggie watched as Julie stiffened slightly.

Terry smiled, trying to put her at ease. "I really am Dr. Terrence Malone, from Manchester University, but this is my niece, Margaret Malone, and this is her brother, Daniel. And this is Bobby Gonzalez, Maggie's boyfriend." He took a breath. "There's no easy way to say this. Maggie and Danny are your half brother and half sister, and they have waited a long time to tell you their mother's story."

Julie's hand flew to her mouth, and then she clutched at her chest, as if gasping for a breath. "Oh my God," she whispered. She started to cry softly, and opened her purse and fumbled for a tissue. "I'm sorry. I'm…in shock."

Maggie wasn't sure what to do. "We're sorry. Circumstances meant we didn't know how to prepare you or warn you."

Maggie found it difficult not to stare at her, seeing all the ways they looked alike, how Tam looked like their mother.

Terry added in a soft voice, "We didn't even know if you wanted to be found, so to speak, if you were ever curious about your biological mother."

Julie dabbed at her eyes again, then smiled, then started crying again. "These are happy tears. I have always wondered, even thought of going to Vietnam to search for her, but assumed there would be no way to trace her, especially because of the war. I'm amazed, stunned really, that you could have found me. How? Tell me how…and where is my mother?"

Danny said, softly, "She passed away, but she looked for you until the day she died. She never gave up on finding you. She loved you. And now we've found you."

Maggie jumped in, the words tumbling out. "She even named you Tam. It means *heart* in Vietnamese. You were her heart. Very much so. Her beloved Tam."

Maggie watched as the words sank in. Julie again fumbled in her bag for a tissue. "I always thought, I…dreamed of meeting her."

"We have pictures," Maggie said. "And you have us. Danny and me. We have been through so much to find you."

"God," Julie said. "I have a sister." Again she started laughing and crying. "I must seem crazy. I'm just overwhelmed. We even look alike."

"I know." Maggie smiled at her and reached out for Julie's hand. "Sister." And then she looked at Danny. "Brother."

"And I'm your uncle," Terry said. "I've been looking for you for over twenty years."

"To think I am so loved." Julie wiped her eyes. "Tell me about her, about this search. Tell me everything. My God. My name is Tam," she said slowly.

Maggie looked at Danny and then at Terry. "We were wondering…we have a suite upstairs. We thought we'd order some room service and sit where it's quiet, and we can tell you the whole story. We have some things to show you."

"Of course, of course. That would be better. Let's go." She smiled at them. They all stood and Terry paid the bill.

As they left, Maggie came over to Julie and gave her a hug. "I am so glad to meet you. Oh shit, now *I'm* crying."

They all laughed a little uneasily and headed out of the bar toward the elevators. Maggie wished she could preserve this moment. This moment when they had found their sister and she was happy and laughing and crying, and it was all beautiful. She knew they would never be this way, this precise way, ever again. Maybe someday they would all smile and laugh together, but once they told her the whole story, it would forever be tinged with death and sadness and horror.

They rode in the elevator to their floor, and walked down the hall to their suite. Once inside, Terry asked Julie, "Can we order you something to eat? Something to drink?"

"Only if you're all eating. Otherwise, I'll be fine. I'd like a soda if you have it."

Terry nodded and went over to the minibar. He got her a soda, and a scotch for himself. He handed Danny a mini-bottle of bourbon, and then brought Maggie a can of ginger ale. Bobby shook his head. "Nothing for me."

The five of them sat around a coffee table, Julie and Danny in chairs, Maggie and Bobby on a love seat, and Terry on another.

"Okay, here goes," Maggie began. "Our mother never intended for you to be adopted at all. Our father, who was a soldier who married our mother, spent thousands of dollars to smuggle you out of Vietnam along with her. Your papers were forged by a French priest, and you and our mother, Mai, were supposed to arrive and Uncle Terry was to collect you both and keep you in Boston until my dad was through with his situation there and in Laos."

"Mai," Julie smiled. "Her name was Mai."

Danny reached into his back pocket and flipped open his wallet. "Here's a picture of her."

He passed the wallet to Julie. She took her index finger and traced it along the photo. "Mai." She stared at it for a long moment. "I look like her, don't I?"

Danny nodded and Julie handed him back his wallet.

Maggie went on, "So that was what was supposed to happen, that was the plan. The two of you were to stay together. But—" Maggie stopped. How would they ever explain all this?

Terry continued for Maggie, "As you know, the war was a complex failure for the United States, and there were certain persons with a vested interest in making sure you and Mai didn't stay together."

"Our mother witnessed a massacre in Vietnam," Danny interrupted.

"A massacre? Was it My Lai?"

"No," Maggie said. "It was her own small village. But Mom had filmed it. Our father had given her a camera. Two cameras, actually. One an Instamatic type, and the other an actual eight-millimeter movie type. And then a man who participated in the massacre came to find out she had this film. We think Mom was killed for it. We know our father was killed for it."

"What? No... This is...crazy."

"I know this is really, really overwhelming. We just wanted you to know how desperately she loved you. She didn't give you up. You were stolen from her."

"Stolen?"

Danny sighed. "This film has been like the friggin' kiss of death for everyone who's hidden it."

"God…" She leaned back in her chair. "Have you seen this film?"

They all nodded.

"I want to see it."

Bobby exhaled. Maggie looked at him and then at their newfound sister. "Julie, Danny and I have one father, and you have a different one. Your father is on the film. He raped our mother. Which didn't change how she felt about you. You were her heart, her Tam. We don't even know you and we love you, too. You're our sister."

Bobby looked at Julie. "People have died to find you. So before you watch this film, you need to decide if you really want to take the next step. If just knowing that you now have Danny and Maggie and Terry is enough, you don't have to go there. Into that village and that massacre."

"Look," Julie said resolutely. "You don't know much about me, but I can assure you, honestly, that I am the type of person who would rather face things head on than hide from them."

"But this is heavy," Danny said. "And as your brother, I gotta protect you, just like I protect Maggie."

She turned her head toward him. "Is that what happened to your face? Protecting this secret?"

"Yes."

"Then I have to see it. Please. I'm a very strong person."

Maggie looked to her family for approval, and they all looked back at her with expressions of people who knew what the right thing was to do. She nodded and stood, crossing the room to her adjoining bedroom. She returned a minute later with Hop's VCR tape, which she had stored in her room's safe.

"Julie," she said. "Just know that we're very sorry."

Maggie popped the tape into the VCR and turned on the TV. There was no sound, of course. The screen flickered and then the images emerged from the darkness. Figures ran from fires, and every time a grenade went off, the world as Mai had filmed it was illuminated. Maggie thought it was the illumination of death. Somehow the silent screams of her mother's people, of *their* mother's people, were even more haunting.

And then came that moment in the film. Two men approaching the hiding spot. A flash of light. The man turned his face.

The burn.

The expression of cold delight.

Calhoun.

"Oh my God," Julie whispered in shock. She began trembling, and Terry jumped from his seat and knelt on the carpet next to her.

"If we could have, Julie, we would have spared you this. But people have died because of this film."

She leaned her elbows on her knees, and cradled her head in her hands. "I needed to know. That's my mother."

"That was you, too. Julie, you were in that hiding spot. Along with your grandmother."

"I—I was in there with them?"

Terry nodded.

"I lived through this…genocide?"

"We're so sorry," Maggie said.

Julie lifted her head. "My mother. My poor, poor mother." She looked at Danny, her eyes determined, thoughtful. "Do you have a picture of your father in your wallet?"

Danny pulled his wallet out again and flipped past a couple of pictures behind the one of Mai. "Here," he said to her. "This was when he was flying for Air America."

He handed Julie the picture.

"The man of my dreams," she whispered.

"What do you mean?" Maggie asked her.

"Every once in a while, I have a dream of an American man. He's holding me and I am playing with his dog tags. I always wondered if that man was my father or if he was a soldier who rescued me before I was adopted. It's him. The man of my lone dream of Vietnam."

Chapter Thirty-Seven

Saigon, August 1973

Jimmy and Mai ate breakfast in their apartment in Saigon. Just as Jimmy knew she would, she had turned it into a home. She'd tucked little statues on the shelves he'd made, and she had hung red scarves and tapestries on the walls.

Nearly five months before, Mai had found Con, courtesy of a bar girl he liked a lot. It had been so long since Jimmy had seen his Mai. Jimmy would never forget walking into the apartment that night. Mai had hidden in the bedroom. Then when his back had been turned, she'd simply stepped out and waited for him to notice her.

He'd been across the room in three strides and had grabbed her so fiercely, he'd been afraid he'd crushed her. He'd felt an ache that had started in the pit of his stomach and radiated down to his groin. He would have made love to her right there if Con hadn't been in the room.

"Tam?" he'd asked, kissing every inch of Mai's face.

"Sleeping on your bed."

He'd gone to look at the sleeping little angel. He'd come back and said to Con, "How?"

"It wasn't me, man. She found *me*."

Jimmy looked at Mai and felt a burning in his throat. He never wanted to be separated from her again.

Now, anytime that he flew, he had Con stay with her, or the old woman from downstairs would keep her company. He and Mai were both changed. He was more somber. He still brought her candy and still tried to make her laugh, but he would find his mind going round and round with things at all hours of the night. Before, he would see Mai whenever he could get away. Now, she lived with him and he was responsible for her. She had lost her entire village.

Mai was also different. She would sometimes stare at Tam or look out the window, somewhere else, somewhere he would never see, he knew. He tried to find out how she had escaped the battle at her village, how long she had hidden with Tam, but she refused to talk about it. She was superstitious, and he figured she thought it would be bad to speak of the dead, of that horrible night, so he let her be.

Over breakfast, Mai smiled at him. "I make something special for dinner tonight."

"And why am I so lucky?"

"Because. We celebrate another flight A-okay."

He smiled. He loved the little bits of American slang that peppered her speech. Once, he had tried to explain hippies and the protests back home. He'd told her that the hippies didn't like "the man"—and that, frankly, he was starting to hate the man, the government, and most especially Richard

Nixon. Then he'd told her about clashes between protestors and "the pigs." Later that night, with Con over for dinner, she'd said, in classic Mai fashion, "Jimmy tell me the hippies do not like livestock." She always made him smile.

"An A-okay flight is a great reason for a celebration," Jimmy told her.

"You watch Tam while I go to market."

Tam was sleeping in a crib he'd bought.

Mai stood and went over to the canvas bag she used to carry fruit and vegetables in. He could see how much she was learning to love the city. It was crowded and noisy, but it also offered a huge variety of food.

Mai left and Jimmy cleaned up the dishes, rinsing them in the sink. He poured himself a second cup of tea. He was getting used to tea. She would make him coffee, but he found that he enjoyed the ritual of tea.

Then he sat and read a newspaper—an Australian one that an Aussie reporter had given him, a buddy of his he sometimes drank with.

After about twenty minutes, he decided to check on Tam. It wasn't like her to sleep in. As a matter of fact, Tam usually awoke before dawn and giggled and babbled until he brought her into their bed and played with her. She liked to grab at his face, and she would clutch fists full of Mai's hair to wake her.

"Hey, shorty," he whispered, touching her face. Her cheeks were burning. "Christ!" He lifted her up. Her entire body was so hot, it terrified him. He tried to rouse her, "Tam, wake up! Come on! It's me, your Jimmy-uncle. Come on!"

His heart raced. He wasn't sure if he'd ever felt fear like this before. Clutching her to his chest, he ran out of their apartment and down one floor to the old grandma. He banged on her door and the wizened woman opened it. She spoke very little English, so he simply thrust Tam at her and grabbed the woman's gnarled hand to make her touch Tam's face.

The old woman clucked and the two of them rushed back upstairs. Once in the apartment, the woman ran cold water from the faucet and wet towels. She gestured for Jimmy to hold Tam on his lap while she applied cool compresses. Tam whimpered and Jimmy's eyes watered. He hated seeing the kid like this.

Again, the old woman made hand gestures for Jimmy to keep applying the cool compresses and she turned to leave.

"You can't go, please. I don't know what to do," he pleaded.

She signaled him in a way to imply he be patient and she disappeared out into the hallway. She came back five minutes later with some kind of concoction in a brown glass bottle. Jimmy eyed it suspiciously, but he felt relieved when she brought it to Tam's lips. Tam took a few very feeble sips. Now she was shivering a bit. The old woman took off the compresses and went to the bedroom and brought back a blanket. They wrapped Tam in it tightly, swaddling her, and then the old woman showed Jimmy how to hold her, with her cheek against Jimmy's chest near his heart. She gestured for him to rock and pace.

Rock and pace he did. He felt as if he walked the equivalent of ten miles back and forth, back and forth. But eventually, he looked down, and Tam's fever seemed to have broken. She was languid and tired, but she grabbed at his chin and even gave him a smile.

"Baby girl, that's the sweetest smile I've ever seen," he whispered.

The old woman came over to him and kissed him on both cheeks. Then she left and it was just him and Tam. He held her, afraid to let her go. A swift-moving rain cloud came and drenched their Saigon street. It brought an unusual coolness, and he stood by the open window and held her, feeling a breeze on his face.

Tam cooed.

"You and me, we gotta stick together. Don't ever scare me like that again." He leaned down and kissed her nose, and Tam laughed and batted at his cheek with her chubby fist.

"You and me and Mai. Forever."

Chapter Thirty-Eight

Maggie's face was wet with tears. "You remember our dad?"

Julie nodded. "Like a snapshot in my head. I always wondered who he was. Sometimes I wondered if I just imagined him. I have bits of memories. Fragments that come to me usually at night."

"Do you remember our mother?" Maggie asked.

"I think so. I have that memory of your father, and then one or two of her humming to me. Speaking to me in a language I don't understand. I don't speak Vietnamese. I tried to study it for a while, but found, though I grasped French and Italian quickly, that I was...I don't know, stuck every time I tried to learn Vietnamese."

"Trauma." Terry said it resolutely.

"I think so," Julie said. "I was obviously ripped away from her. I've cut off all memory of that world. Of what happened to me. When I came here to survive, I must have closed that off. I even went to a psychologist who tried hypnosis. I just could never recover more than fragments, snapshots. Frozen moments in time."

"Julie," Terry said, rising from the floor. "Now you know why we weren't sure how to break all this to you at once. And now you know how dangerous that film is."

She took a deep breath. "I wish I could say that I'm shocked. I'm devastated, but that's not the same thing. I'm overwhelmed. I am totally horrified, but is he capable of something like that?... I'm ashamed to say I think so."

Maggie grabbed Bobby's hand. She felt for Julie. For Tam. For this ghost girl who was now a woman.

Julie reached down to the coffee table and took a sip of her soda. "My father never spent much time with me. I always felt he was avoiding me. My mother thought he was avoiding her. We were a classic Washington family. Split between two cities. Basically, my adoptive mother and I stayed in Indiana and he lived in Washington. Later on, there were rumors, just the barest of hints, of other women. Then he became born again and that was the end of those rumors. But born again or not, he was still cold and distant. I think I eventually studied eastern philosophy as a search for my heritage and also to reject the label Christian. I always felt like if he was an example of Christianity, I wanted no part of it."

She sighed. "He met his current wife at a political fundraiser, though they were just friends, he claims. He served my mother divorce papers shortly thereafter. Then I never saw him. Worse, he started dating the new woman, and she had a lot of money, a lot of connections. He used her family's very fancy, very tough, very Beltway lawyer to negotiate a divorce settlement. It was brutal for my mother. The settlement wasn't quite so awful as to make him look politically heartless, but it was tough enough that she needed to get a job, although she'd been a homemaker her whole life. She had to sell our house and move to a very, very modest ranch."

"Prick," Danny said.

Julie smiled. "I can tell we're going to get along just fine." She gave a quick laugh. "He paid for half of my college tuition. My mom was supposed to pay the other half, but she really didn't have it. He never sent me any money for books, nothing extra. Even my birthday was celebrated with a perfunctory card with a nominal check and even more nominal sentiment.

"I had a partial scholarship and worked two jobs, and my mom sent me what she could. But his new children have had the silver spoon in their mouths and then some. Platinum spoons. When my mother got breast cancer, I contacted him. I was nineteen. He told me, coldly, that if she died, he expected me to sell the house we lived in and use that to fund the rest of my education and to get a fresh start. And he didn't think it would be wise for me to spend holidays with his family because it was just difficult for his wife and children. I was, quote, hard to explain to the kids. When my mother died, there were no flowers, no calls, no nothing. I buried her alone."

"How has this not come out in the media? I mean, usually they find out what bastards these guys are," Terry said. "Newt Gingrich served his ex-wife divorce papers in her hospital room after her mastectomy. That came out in the press. And people rightfully hated him."

Julie shrugged. "You underestimate the power of the Calhouns. They're friends with Saudi princes and are on the boards of many of the most powerful corporations in the world. My grandfather was an assistant director of the CIA, and even in the little realm of our family before my parents were divorced, he was so controlling that I was terrified of him. I remember him once slapping my hand so hard it was red for hours. I was seven and had dared to stick my finger in the icing of my birthday cake. My grandmother was worse. She urged me to make my eyes look more American, by drawing my eyeliner a certain way. They are surrounded by people who fawn over their power. I have no doubt they control their dynasty by whatever means necessary. People know they're a tough clan, but they wrap it up in a ribbon of Sunday-morning Bible thumping, and I think people are fooled."

Bobby wrapped an arm around Maggie. She leaned against him. For all she had been through, sewing up bullet wounds and cleaning the beer and slop of a barroom floor to earn her allowance, it had all been enveloped in the embrace of a father who loved her fiercely—and a brother who would see this whole thing through to the end, even if it meant losing his own life.

"What about your mother?" Maggie asked.

Julie smiled, and Maggie could see her emotionally relax into her memories. "She was truly wonderful. I lost her way too soon. She was really intimidated by the machine of the Calhouns. They tried to tell her how to dress, what to say, how to worship, even. When my parents were first married, my mother attended a lovely Lutheran church. But there weren't enough connections there to satisfy my grandparents' plans for their young, politically ambitious son. My grandparents picked my parents' churches from then on. My grandfather used to joke about the Cadillac ratio. He said to count them all up, and if there were more Cadillacs than any other type of car, that church was a networking place."

"How'd your father even marry her?" Maggie asked.

Julie pursed her lips. "Honestly? I think she had one specific trait he wanted. She was pliable."

Maggie thought of how she and Danny and Mai would make the trek to St. Patrick's. Mai's jelly jars of holy water. The experience may have been disjointed, but it was very real.

"My mother," Julie continued, "was the kind of person all my friends wanted to be around. It wasn't that she was one of those moms who tried to be cool or hip. It was almost as if she was the antithesis of that, which made her special. She loved nothing more than having a house full of girls, her whipping up brownies or something. She remembered all the details of their lives and always seemed genuinely fascinated about what we were doing, encouraging us to pursue our dreams. She used to make shadow boxes."

"What are those?" Danny asked.

"They're like display cases. You can make arrangements, like of photos and memories. She once made one of a vacation she and I took to Florida. She arranged seashells in the box, and then photos of us, a little bottle she filled with sand. They were really pretty, and she did a box for every year of my life, all the little things you save—ticket stubs, and shiny rocks I gave her when I was little, telling her they were diamonds. I felt so absolutely loved by her."

"I'm so grateful you had that," Maggie said. "We had that. I wish you could have known our mother."

"I've lost two mothers."

The five of them traded stories until long after midnight. Finally, Danny said, "The film. We want this to be over, Julie. We want our lives back the way they were. Can you arrange a private meeting with your father? We just want to make some kind of deal. The film for our safety. A dead man's switch. If anything happens to us, the film is released. We stay alive. The film stays buried."

Maggie looked at her brother. She knew he was lying. Hop had had a dead man's switch, and look what had happened to him. She exchanged glances with Bobby, hoping he could figure out a way for them to do what they needed without Danny killing the senator.

Julie thought for a moment. "I'll tell him that a reporter from the *Washington Post* is onto a story about my mother, and also my adoption. I'll tell him that we'd best not speak over the phone, and I'll say I want to meet with him alone, no security. At my house."

"Any time. Any place," Danny said.

Terry nodded. "And now we should all get some rest."

"I hate to leave you all, but I'd better go. I'll call you here when I have a meeting set up."

They all stood, and one by one, Julie hugged each of them. When she got to Danny, she put her fingers tenderly on his face, where the bruising was dark and mottled. "I'm so sorry."

"Well, we Malones are tough."

"I hope so, going up against the Calhouns."

She kissed Terry on the cheek and then left the suite. As soon as she was gone, Maggie turned to Danny and said, "We found her. Uncle Terry was right. We can bring him down. We don't have to kill him to do it."

"I'm not going to kill him," Danny said, his voice flat.

"Bullshit." Maggie walked over to him until she was a foot away and said, "Give me the Glock."

"No. I said I wasn't going to kill him. But that doesn't mean I'm walking into a meeting with that bastard unarmed."

"She may have just met you and Uncle Terrence may not have seen us in years, but I know how your mind works."

"Then you know to back off. We do the dead man's switch."

Maggie turned on her heel and walked into her bedroom. *A dead man's switch.* She just prayed at the end she could keep her brother from being a real dead man. Or one doomed to prison.

Chapter Thirty-Nine

Idaho, December 2004

Jimmy found the mailbox on a rural delivery route in Idaho. It was pretty country out here, he'd give it that. Wide open spaces. Mountains. A good place to go if you didn't want anyone to find you. And one of the friendliest states for gun owners. He didn't kid himself that he might be walking into an ambush.

He drove his rented car down a long dirt road. Snow drifts sat to his left and right, and a bitter wind kicked up the odd leaf, making the trees bend. Jimmy banked to the left, and there stood the cabin on a river. From what he'd heard, Mike Flynn—now Ted Smith—liked to fly-fish. He also liked to be alone. And according to the owner of the lone liquor store in the town ten miles away—if you could even call it a town—he liked his Johnnie Walker Red.

Jimmy parked his car, turned off the engine, checked the gun in the holster around his ankle and patted the one in the waistband of his pants. He climbed out of his car, pulled his jacket tighter around himself, and, much as he expected, was greeted by a man wielding a shotgun who stood on the porch of the cabin.

"Can't you read the No Trespassing signs?" the man said. He was thin, his face gaunt and wrinkled. Jimmy knew they were contemporaries, but the years hadn't been kind to Mike Flynn—not that he deserved them to be. He wore a plaid flannel shirt and a pair of brown canvas overalls and hip waders.

"I can read them," Jimmy said.

"Then get off my land."

"Don't you want to know who I am, or who I'm looking for?"

Mike Flynn narrowed his eyes. He leveled the shotgun at Jimmy's chest.

"You blow me away and I won't be able to call my friend in exactly a half hour." Jimmy looked at his watch. "If he doesn't hear from me, your whereabouts and name goes to the feds and the media. They'll pick apart your life like vultures, Mike."

Jimmy watched the man's reaction when he used the guy's real name. Flynn's eyelids fluttered for a second.

"If you're not with the government, then who the hell are you?"

"A father."

"I don't follow, and I guess I just as soon blow a hole in you."

"My wife's daughter—" Jimmy found his voice quavered slightly, anger tinged with grief. "In my heart, she's my daughter. She was there when you massacred that village. And all

I want to know now is what happened, who ordered it, and if you're sorry. And then I'll be on my way."

Flynn's eyes, bloodshot and pale blue, narrowed. "Why shouldn't I kill you?"

"Because you have so much blood on your hands already. And you're closer to death than life, my friend. Each day brings you closer and closer and you know you're not forgiven. Not yet."

"I was following orders."

"Whose?"

Jimmy watched as Mike Flynn wrestled with the truth. Finally, he said, "Calhoun. But my guess is you come all this way to find me, you already knew that."

"And why? What set him off?"

"I don't know. When we got to that village, we were supposed to be looking for a cache of weapons, for hidden NVA. Something. But once we were there, he started going haywire. He was shooting at anything. And then a few villagers resisted. We'd lost a bunch of guys in another battle over a stupid patch of land none of us gave a shit about. So the resistance pissed us off. The heat. The fucking mosquitoes. The constant dampness of our socks. The misery. You had to be there to understand."

"I was there," Jimmy said flatly. "I know about misery. But I also know about women and children and old men, and people who didn't deserve to die. You want to kill me, a retired old soldier, fine. But those people…they didn't deserve any of it."

"We were just boys, for God's sake. We were like a powder keg and Calhoun lit the match. We just lost it. When one of the villagers fired a gun, a guy in the platoon said something about how he wasn't leaving in a body bag. And then the shooting got out of hand."

Flynn lowered his shotgun. "I know for a fact I killed women." He looked at Jimmy, his eyes pleading for forgiveness. "I was firing...I don't even know what at. Then in the middle of it, I stopped. I just...stood there, frozen. I was watching it all around me, like in slow motion. I saw two little children lying on the ground. And I saw men lighting fires. Lots of fire. And Calhoun was the scariest of them all."

"Why?"

"'Cause me, me and my guys, we went crazy you know? I snapped. I sat down at some point and just started crying, bullets whizzing by my head. But Calhoun, he was carrying this out like it was a goddamn execution. Cold. Calculating. Leaving nothing. Not even the farm animals."

"He left a witness."

"Your daughter?"

"My wife and daughter, actually."

"Did you come here to kill me?"

"I came here for answers. But eventually, I'm going to kill Calhoun." Jimmy stated this as if it were fact, a foregone conclusion.

"You asked me if I was sorry."

"Are you?"

"I've sucked on the barrel of my gun more times than I can count."

"So why don't you do it?"

"Fear. Of what comes next. Of meeting God. And he's

going to send me to hell. And hell? It's like the village every night. That's what I think hell is."

"You're probably right." Jimmy had traveled a long way to hear Flynn's story only to realize he was better off letting Flynn torture himself rather than Jimmy putting him out of his misery.

"Tell your wife I'm sorry. Your daughter, too."

"It's too late for my wife. I'm trying to make sure it's not too late for my daughter."

Jimmy turned and opened his car door. "One more thing, Flynn."

"Yeah?"

"You changed your name. You came to fucking Idaho. You live off the grid. Are you afraid of the ghosts of Vietnam or Calhoun?"

Mike leaned his shotgun against his front door, then he took two steps and rested his hands on the railing of his porch.

"One by one, we're all dead. I'm the only thing standing between that man and the White House. What do *you* think I'm afraid of?"

"I thought so," Jimmy said, ducking his head down and climbing back in his car.

Now he and everyone he loved stood between Calhoun and the Oval Office.

Chapter Forty

Bobby had a very bad feeling about the meeting. Julie said her father was annoyed at her for contacting him. He wanted to send one of his top aides in his place, but she was resolute that it had to be him, alone. So he was supposed to show at nine o'clock. Bobby looked at his watch. He had ten minutes.

Julie lived in a town house in Georgetown. She had sold her mother's home like Calhoun had suggested, and she had invested wisely. A life-insurance policy on her mother she hadn't even known about had meant she could afford this place, and full professorship at Georgetown meant she could keep it.

The place was furnished simply, and Bobby mused, with the love of her adoptive mother evident. Most of the main pieces appeared to be family heirlooms, heavy and wooden and nicked and scratched, but still carefully polished. Everything else reflected Julie's love of Vietnam and eastern philosophy. It reminded him a little of Maggie's place. Buddha masks and statues vied with porcelain vases. Books filled every shelf.

The four of them waited in Julie's study. It adjoined her formal living room, where, she said, she would settle her father in a chair and then they would confront him.

Bobby kept looking at Danny, whose dark eyes were intense. Bobby, clean and sober all these years, for once wished someone was wasted—he would have preferred Danny have the glazed-over OxyContin look. Bobby thought that look was more peaceful, easier to manage perhaps.

Maggie hadn't slept at all the previous night. She was always thin, but when she didn't sleep, she looked even more so, like a sparrow.

Terry, meanwhile, looked worse than all of them. Bobby figured all his emotions had been stirred up, his unrequited love for Mai, his brother's death, the lost years. Jimmy had purposely kept him from Maggie and Danny this whole time as part of his theory that it was better that the keepers of the secret stay apart from one another, each man guarding his share.

Ten minutes later, almost to the second, Julie's doorbell ring. They could hear her heels clicking on the hardwood floors, and they heard murmurs as she ushered her father into the living room. Bobby had noted how she didn't call him *Father*. She referred to him as either the Senator or the man who'd adopted her. She didn't even address the fact that his DNA ran through her veins.

They had planned on waiting two minutes, and Bobby looked at his watch again, expecting the others to give the signal. His shirt was sticking to him, his palms sweating. He kept looking at Danny and hoped to hell he could keep a lid on this meeting.

Bobby finally gave the signal, and Terry walked through the door first, followed by Maggie, Danny and then Bobby bringing up the rear.

"What the hell is going on?" Calhoun blustered from the wingback chair where he sat. Bobby thought he looked just as he did on television. His haircut was as impeccably short as a cop's, his shoes shined to a glossy reflection, his suit crisp.

Maggie went and stood next to Julie. Danny took his place next to both women. They waited a minute, to see if Calhoun understood.

Bobby watched as the senator clenched his jaw.

"Julie, I demand to know what in heaven's name is going on."

Julie wrapped her arm around Maggie's waist. "My name is Tam," she whispered. "And I've seen the film. So are you going to kill me, too?"

But Calhoun wasn't ready to knock his king down and accept checkmate. "What are you talking about? Who are these people?"

Terry stepped forward. "These three are Mai Malone's children. I'm Mai's brother-in-law."

"Julie," her father intoned, "I demand to know what lies you've been fed. You're my daughter, and these...these people clearly have gotten you confused."

"I have never even been to your home," Julie said, her voice quavering. "I am not your daughter. Why did you even bring me home?"

They had made several copies of the tape and had mailed

them to themselves, and to Terry's office, to his lawyer. One was hidden in Julie's bedroom. Julie crossed to a large wooden wall unit and opened a cabinet that revealed a small television. She put the tape into the VCR. The tape began to play.

Bobby watched Calhoun, who sat quite calmly in his chair.

"What does this prove? I can't even see what's on that tape. It's filmed in the dark. It could be anything. Anyone."

Danny snapped, "Wait!"

And so, in silence, they waited for the moment of truth. And then it came. The grenade, the illuminated sky, the soldier turned. The burn on his neck. The expression in his eyes.

Danny wheeled around. "Yeah. We have the tape. The tape you've wondered about for all these years. The tape you killed my father for. How do you like a grenade being tossed into your foxhole, Calhoun? Huh?"

Julie approached Calhoun. "Why? Why did you bring me here? Why didn't you let me go with my mother? With Mai? It's obvious you've never loved me."

He sat completely still. "I'm not going to address any of these insane allegations. That tape could be a forgery. So if that's all…"

His arrogance, Bobby thought, was overwhelming, and he knew it was enough to pull the pin on Danny's grenade. And just as he'd expected, Danny's Glock came out. He strode over to the chair and aimed the gun right at Calhoun's temple.

"Answer her. She deserves that much."

Calhoun appeared to weigh his options. Finally, he spoke to Julie, acting as if he didn't even notice the gun in Danny's hand.

"I thought I would kill two birds with one stone. Your

mother back home couldn't have children. I, apparently, could. When I realized that Jimmy Malone was bound and determined to get that woman out of Saigon, and you along with her, I decided to keep my eye on things. I wasn't sure that you were mine. That woman could have been a whore. But I thought I would make sure that you didn't pop into my life as a political surprise someday. I also figured you'd be leverage. I didn't know about the tape until later. If she had destroyed that tape, if she had let it go, she'd be alive today."

"Let it go?" Maggie shrieked. "Let it go? This wasn't a bad relationship or an indiscretion. You committed genocide in that village. Let it go? Our entire family, our mother's entire Vietnamese ancestry was killed in one night."

Calhoun smirked slightly. "It was war. Even that tape has no context. There are no surviving platoon members. We were under heavy fire."

Bobby couldn't believe that was how Calhoun was going to play this. He didn't plead for his life, or show any kind of remorse. Instead, he was justifying it.

"Danny," Bobby intoned. "Put the gun away. You got your answers. We just put the tape on the eleven o'clock news and let the media fry him. There'll be congressional hearings. Maybe he'll do some time like Calley. But walk away, Danny."

"If you shoot me, son, my bodyguards will come in here and kill you all."

Danny suddenly lost it. He pistol-whipped the senator. "Don't call me your fucking son!" he screamed. Calhoun groaned and put his hand to his cheek.

Maggie soothed, "Danny, we have our sister now."

He looked over at Tam. She was crying. "He's not worth it."

Calhoun stood. "If I'm not out of this town house in ten minutes, my security detail will come in." He still clutched his cheek and his voice was less powerful now.

"The tape is going to the *Washington Post,*" Julie said. "Your life will be ruined."

"Well," he said. "I suppose I had better go meet with my team to determine how we'll respond."

Bobby watched Danny warily. He didn't like the look on his face. "Okay now, everyone, let him leave."

Danny looked at Bobby. At that moment, there was a knock on the door.

"My security," the senator said. He stood and adjusted his tie.

And then Bobby stood helplessly as three shots were fired in the living room of Dr. Julie Calhoun's home.

Chapter Forty-One

"Everyone freeze," came the command.

Maggie was screaming, Julie was kneeling on the floor. Bobby had drawn his own gun. "I'm reaching for my badge," he said.

And Danny Malone looked at the barrel of his Glock.

It hadn't gone off.

"Uncle Terry!" Maggie screamed. Julie had his head in her lap and she was sobbing. Terry was barely breathing.

Terry had drawn a gun, which Danny had never known he'd had, and had fired one shot into the senator's chest. Security had burst into the room, shot Terry twice, and now the two sides were in a standoff.

"I'm a cop," Bobby said from across the room. "NYPD. This was a family dispute."

The security still had their guns drawn and were calling for backup and the police. Danny threw his Glock on the floor and went to his two sisters.

"Uncle Terry," Maggie said as she knelt beside Julie. "Call

an ambulance," she begged, looking up at one of the security guards.

"Already did," he said.

"Uncle Terry, why?" Maggie leaned down and put her cheek to his.

"Let…me…go to Mai," he gasped.

Danny held his uncle's hand. "It's finished now, Uncle Terry. Go to her. Go to a good rebirth."

Julie leaned down and kissed his forehead. "Go to her."

And with that, they watched as their uncle drew his last breath. He shuddered once, groaned and was gone.

Within minutes, the place was swarming with cops. Danny was grateful that Bobby was there. He talked cop-speak. Officers two-deep gathered around the television as the film was played time and time again.

Danny looked over at Calhoun, who had fallen to the ground in a heap. He had no chance for a good rebirth. No chance at heaven. An unrepentant devil to the end.

Danny and Bobby tried to get Maggie and Julie to leave Uncle Terry's side and sit down. Someone in the kitchen was making coffee. Both women were in shock. Maggie was shivering. And neither wanted to leave Terry's body.

"I want to stay with him," Maggie told Danny. "I won't leave him."

He squatted down to look her in the eyes. "This isn't Uncle Terry. It's just his body. And it's going to get cold, and they're going to want to do an autopsy and get him out of here. But we'll make sure he gets rice and coins for his journey? Okay?"

She threw her arms around his neck and started crying

harder than he had ever seen her cry. Her right cheek was smeared with Terry's blood.

Julie was crying, too, and he motioned for her to come over to them. "Come on, Julie."

She made her way to them and the three siblings held each other. Danny's curiosity about how she felt about her father being shot was soon answered.

"He deserved it," she said.

Danny nodded. He had a shoulder for each of them, and the pieces of him that felt oddly missing were found. Maybe he had always known about Tam. Maybe she had always been there, whispering for them to come find her. Like some giant cosmic game of hide and seek between a brother and his sisters.

Chapter Forty-Two

The fallout of the murder of Senator Calhoun was a deafening cacophony. Bobby hadn't seen anything quite like it before, but he supposed that Washington's next scandal was right around the corner. The next on-her-knees intern, the next murderer cloaked in the American flag.

For three weeks, the story was front-page headlines and the lead on the nightly news. It had it all: sex, scandal, politics, cruelty, operatic betrayals, a beautiful woman torn from her child, a love affair, unrequited love. The pundits had a field day with every angle of the story covered, and major papers like the *New York Times* and the *Washington Post* had investigative pieces seeking to uncover more of the truth.

Ballistics cleared Bobby and Danny—their guns were not responsible for either death. And in the end, the story was simply the truth. Terry had shot Calhoun in revenge for what he had done to Mai, and security had killed Terrence.

The film of the massacre was played repeatedly on the news and on talk shows, with experts analyzing it, freezing frames and blowing them up. The split second when Calhoun turned around on the film, his face illuminated in its cold-blooded fury, the telltale burn creeping up from under his collar, was the new face of Calhoun. For the rest of time, Bobby knew, he'd never be remembered as the smiling senator from Indiana with his slick responses and powerful family. He would be a murderer. A massacre leader. A killer. And Bobby was glad for that. Tam deserved that. Mai deserved it.

Pieces of the story, Bobby realized, would probably never be known. For that, they'd need to resurrect Jimmy Malone and ask him about all the secrets, all the blind turns in the maze. Like the winding Ho Chi Minh trail, Bobby wasn't sure where it all led, through grasses and hills and rice paddies. It was a dangerous path, and he was glad they were now out in the open, even if the glare was bright and exhausting for a while.

Julie took a leave of absence from Georgetown as talk of congressional hearings swirled. The three siblings stuck close together, and she gradually preferred her given name, Tam. She came to New York, and holed up with Maggie and Danny in a rented apartment, trying to lose herself in a city that generally seemed to leave famous faces alone. The Twilight continued running under Tony T., and Maggie was contemplating an even bigger offer for the bar—no doubt driven by the newfound fame of its owners.

For Bobby, and perhaps for the Malone siblings, they derived some of their greatest peace and satisfaction from the truth finally being told, the countless sins of the Calhouns, like a grenade, bringing everything to light. Somehow, in all the death and murder and lies, the things that infuriated Bobby the most were the most personal grenades of all. He liked seeing Mrs. Calhoun, the matriarch with her white hair and perfect pearls, exposed for the heartless woman she was. When more details of the first marriage and divorce of the senator became known, when there was no stopping the feeding frenzy, the things done to the first Mrs. Calhoun and to Tam were worse, in some ways, than murder. The press was on the story like sharks around chum.

The Calhouns had at first tried to milk the story of the senator bringing this child home from Vietnam, embracing the people of the war he'd fought in. Their attempts failed. The Calhouns became possibly the most hated people in America, though the present Mrs. Calhoun, who had never had the motherless Tam to her home, even after her adoptive mother died when Tam was just nineteen, was a close second. He heard she stopped lunching in Washington, and was packing her things and hoping to head to Malibu for a fresh start, but he doubted she would ever rise above the stench of her own cruelty.

Christmas came. Bobby proposed to Maggie, putting the ring inside a *gao*. She said yes. Then New Year's Day arrived and the four of them—Bobby, Maggie, Danny and Tam—decided to visit Con. They had managed to tell their story without putting him in it. He stayed off the grid, but the siblings needed to see him.

They drove through the Jersey countryside and came to the usual turnoffs. Maggie gave directions. Danny and Tam rode in the back. His face had healed nicely. After the story broke, he'd gotten to visit a real doctor, who had said Mag-

gie could have a career in medicine. Bobby had stopped
wondering about booby traps and C-4. Maybe someday Con
would be less paranoid, Bobby thought.

They arrived at the cabin, and Con opened the door before they had even turned off the engine.

Maggie ran from the car and threw her arms around his
neck. Tam and Danny came up more slowly, Tam a little shy.
Bobby turned off the car and followed.

Con broke into a wide grin. "Come here, little Tam. You
don't remember me, but I used to feed you rice and eggs."

Tam moved closer to him and he gave her a bear hug. "I'm
sorry for all you've been through, little Tam." He stepped
back. "You look so like your mother. Come on in."

When they stepped inside, Hop poked his head out from
behind the door.

"Jesus Christ!" Danny hugged him. Bobby just smiled, saying, "I never know what to expect from you guys." And that
was the truth.

"Me and my dogs decided to live off the grid for a while."
He moved over to Tam. "I'm not sure what to say. I wish
we'd been able to find you sooner."

The six of them went over to Con's couches and the fireplace. It was quite cold. Con went and got blankets for everyone to put on their laps to keep warm.

"Let me see the ring, Maggie."

Maggie stuck out her left hand.

"Okay, he's a cop, but we'll let him in the family," Con
joked. "He proved himself. Happy New Year."

They all murmured, "Happy New Year." Tam curled her
legs up beneath her and pulled her blanket up to her neck.

Con stood, "Are you cold, sweetie?" He moved to the fire and tossed on two fresh logs. The blaze burst brighter.

Bobby's eyes drifted to the urn on the mantel. The reason for their visit.

"Con," Maggie began. "We want to put Daddy's ashes at the Wall."

Tam nodded. "On January 31."

"Why then?" Hop asked.

"In Vietnam, it's a day to honor your ancestors," Tam said. "And we want to put Terrence there, too. Even though he's not a veteran, in a way, he's a casualty of the war."

Con looked thoughtful. "All right. Seems I'm going to have to make a trip. We'll all go. Do it right. On the thirty-first."

Chapter Forty-Three

On January 31, Maggie Malone felt her entire world had come full circle. She had lost so much, but gained a sister. And a future husband. And her brother seemed more at peace than she could ever recall. He had stopped running. He drank less and laughed more.

Certain there had to be regulations about leaving human ashes at the Wall, they had decided to divide up the ashes into six plastic containers. They would find a spot at the Wall where they could huddle together, hidden from view of others, and open their containers. In turn, Terrence and Jimmy would forever be commemorated there.

Maggie felt a little sad that the names James M. Malone and Terrence P. Malone weren't on the Wall, nor would they ever be. She would never be able to make a rubbing of their names. Never be able to come and stand in front of their names and pray silently. But then, she felt, they would be part of the entire Wall.

Con and Hop wore their old Vietnam jackets. Maggie

watched as they walked the length of the solemn structure, even more stark in the dead of winter. The temperature was just above zero with the windchill. She had pulled her hair into a ponytail to avoid it blowing all over. Tam had thrown a wool cap over her head. They stamped their feet trying to keep warm, all of them as chubby as penguins in their winter layers, as they looked at the names of the dead.

That's what struck Maggie the most. All those names. All those names of fathers and brothers and sons. Young lives, snuffed out for old men like Calhoun's father playing war games. She imagined her father, Con, as young men, full of the bravado of youth, flying in and out of the jungles as the country of Vietnam disintegrated into madness.

She blinked back tears. Where was the Wall for the Hanh family? For her mother's village? For all the Vietnamese dead? Innocent lives. *America doesn't have a monument for that,* she thought.

Con took off a glove and ran his fingers down rows of names. He walked to the book to find his old platoon, and went there. They let him have his privacy as he stood there talking to the Wall, conversing with the ghosts of old buddies. Maggie wandered off alone to a section of wall, looking at herself in the glass-like marble. She looked like a ghost, a spirit, her features not fully realized in the reflection, just a shadowy spirit. There, she talked to Mai, telling her they would honor her every year on this day.

"I'm sorry," she whispered, "for wondering why you jumped. For being angry that you had left us. I'm sorry I doubted how much we meant to you."

Eventually, they each made their peace and drifted together to the corner of the wall. That seemed as good a place as any.

Danny set down a small jade Buddha on the ground. "This is for our mother." He opened his container of ashes and poured them on the grass, deadened by winter. The wind whipped them away.

Maggie poured hers. And one at a time, their backs to the world, faces reflected in the wall, they bid goodbye to Terrence and Jimmy, the two men who had loved Mai. Every time she thought of her uncle, Maggie still cried. It wasn't that she didn't grieve for her father. She did. But he had been chasing Tam for so long, fighting the fight against Calhoun in foxholes of his own necessity, that she was used to his absence. And now she found him all the braver and more heroic.

When they were done, the six of them formed a huddle, their heads leaning against each other, and they were just silent. In the last months, they had said all there was to say, at least for now, about the journey to find Tam.

Finally, they broke apart. January 31 would always be their day to honor their secret war. They turned and started walking slowly to the end of the Wall. They could see a man coming toward them over a rise, head tucked into his jacket collar. Maggie guessed he was a vet. Who else would come out in this to go to the Wall?

But then she looked closer.

"Oh my God." She fell to her knees as Jimmy Malone strode toward them all.

Maggie felt her face and wondered if her tears would freeze there in the cold. Jimmy started running toward them.

She stood and, with everyone, threw her arms around him, touching him, crying, patting his face.

"Is it really you?" she sobbed.

"It's really me, bright eyes."

"Jesus Christ!" Con shouted. Even Hop welled up.

Tam stood slightly off to the side. Jimmy saw her.

"Tam…child of my heart. Come here."

Maggie watched as Tam went to Jimmy. She was crying, but managed to choke out the words, "The soldier of my dreams."

The two of them stood there holding each other. Jimmy leaned his head back so he could look at her. "Just like Mai. My God, you're the vision of her."

Even the normally stoic Con was by now dabbing at the corners of his eyes. Hop grinned from ear to ear.

Finally, Maggie asked. "How did you pull this off?"

Jimmy smiled, releasing Tam, but keeping an arm around her waist.

"When one of Calhoun's platoon was murdered execution style, I decided I really needed to be off the grid. I faked my own death and thought I'd find Tam when everyone's defenses were down thinking I was gone. I had my lawyer send Calhoun a package with a copy of the film and a letter saying that upon my death, the lawyer had been instructed to return that film to Calhoun. I explained that I wanted my children left in peace, and in the event of my death, I hoped this true dead man's switch would end things."

"But they came after me anyway," Danny said. His eyebrow still had a reddish scar through it where the hair wouldn't grow.

"I know. I'm sorry. I thought I was buying you and Maggie your true freedom from this. When I was sure I could tell Tam the truth without it costing Tam her life, I planned on revealing all the pieces. I didn't trust any of that clan as far as I could throw them. Of course, I hadn't counted on you all figuring it out. I hadn't counted on how much Terry loved Mai. She was easy to love, easy to adore. I knew he felt strongly about her, but I never would have guessed he'd avenge her."

Terrence had been cast by the media as a hero. The university, despite some people's protests that they were honoring a murderer, was planning on building a rose garden in his honor that spring.

"I was just hoping to figure out a way to have Tam with us, and keep us all safe. I never meant for Terry to do what he did," his voice grew solemn. "I never meant for any of this. My plan all along was to keep each part of the puzzle separate. Somehow that seemed safer."

"Daddy," Maggie said. "It's okay. I think he really just wanted to be with her. Once this got all stirred up, I think that was his plan all along. It's why he insisted we bring him."

Jimmy nodded.

"How did you know we'd be here?" Maggie asked.

"Well, in the media frenzy, I figured I'd better fly under the radar. But then I went back to the Twilight around 3:00 a.m. two nights ago. Tony T. told me where you were."

"So now what?" Danny asked.

"Now, we honor our ancestors. Then we never let Tam out of our sight again," he said and winked at her. "And we repair our family. Mai would want us all together."

Maggie looked at the Wall. The marble was so dark and liquid-like, she felt as if she could step through to the other side. She imagined soldiers there, ghosts of child-men forever frozen, never growing old, and she imagined Mai and Terry, hand in hand, gazing at them from beyond.

She turned to her sister. When they looked into each other's eyes, Maggie always felt as if she were seeing a reflection of herself.

She used to feel invisible. A ghost girl in Hell's Kitchen, caught between east and west, Buddha and Jesus, heaven and rebirth.

But not anymore. She took her sister's hand and her brother's, and with Bobby, and Con and Hop and her father, they walked from the Wall, leaving its ghosts of boy soldiers and ancestors in peace.

Tess Hudson is a former blackjack dealer who now resides in Florida. She plays poker regularly and is always hoping for that inside straight. Tess likes martinis, shooting pool and playing chess. She has loved to play cards since she was taught how to play rummy by her grandmother, and since she saw *The Sting*. She has donated her time for years teaching English to refugees and immigrants from Vietnam, Cambodia and recently Brazil. She is currently at work on her next novel, as well as a screenplay. She may be reached at her Web site at www.tesshudson.com.

MIRA®